FIFTEEN DAYS OF SUMMER

By
Becky Perkins

To Janis,
I really hope that you enjoy the book.
Best wishes

For my dad, I hope he would have been proud?

Becky ✕x

Acknowledgements

This all started with a feeling of deep sadness that wouldn't go away and the memory of how to write a story, which grew into something really quite special. I want to thank my husband Simon for being so supportive on my journey back to him; for never doubting, for his eternal belief in me and his unconditional love. Thanks must also go to my lovely Mum for her encouragement and for sharing some of her childhood memories with me and allowing me to bring them to life. To my two beautiful girls who have provided me with such inspiration for the characters, I love you both dearly. Thank you to the people who agreed to read my book in its rawest form, without your input and encouragement I never would have had the confidence to get it published. Finally, thank you to those who have chosen to purchase and read my book, I hope that you enjoy the story as much as I have enjoyed writing it, it has been a real joy.

DAY ONE

The Discovery

It was the start of the school summer holidays and Gerald wasn't going to waste a moment. In search of adventure, he raced from his terraced house in Richmond Street and ran up into the fields near his home. In the distance he could see his favourite tree swing hanging invitingly over the stream. After sprinting towards it, he kicked off his shoes, tugged off his heavily darned socks and jumped on to the gigantic knot which swayed gently in the summer breeze.

Swinging back and forth across the cool stream, basking in the glorious summer heat, Gerald thought of his closest friends; now back in their London homes. Sadness filled his heart as he reflected on their escapades in summers gone by. His life had been so full when they had come to stay with their uncle, just after the war had started. Every day he'd had playmates his own age. It was true friendship, the kind he thought would last a lifetime. When his companions had left Nottinghamshire to go back to London, Gerald feared that he would never see them again. Albert, their uncle, had told him that the boys would re-join him one day, but it had been over two years since Germany had surrendered and the evacuees had not come back. Despite the years passing by, Gerald still held onto the promise of their return.

In the absence of real adventure, his fantastic imagination took on a life of its own, telling elaborate and wonderful stories to anyone who would listen. His tales were so believable that many people were easily convinced.

Weary and embarrassed by his constant romancing, his mother grew frustrated and annoyed with her young son. She knew he craved stimulation and prayed that he'd find new friends to play with and the sooner the better as far as she was concerned.

Gerald stepped down from the swing into the stream, taking in the refreshing feeling as the water ran over his toes. As he paddled in the cool water, he watched the bees amongst the yellow iris', which ran alongside the bank. Bending down to take in the magical scent, he spotted a bright red, white and blue striped insect hidden amongst the undergrowth. He hitched up his short grey trousers and carefully bent down to part the blades of grass shielding the little chap and peered closely at him.

"Hello little fella," he cooed. Gerald was enthralled, he'd seen plenty of brown and green caterpillars and even some brighter ones, when he went for his walks, but he'd never seen a stripy one!

Deciding that this matter warranted an even closer look, he rummaged in his pockets for his treasured magnifying glass, which his Uncle Alan had given him on his fifth birthday. Hovering over the caterpillar's tiny frame, the small magnifier enabled Gerald to see that the creature had black markings around his eyes, making it look like he was wearing glasses. With the exception of the sixteenth, there were black splodges and yellow dots on each and every foot. It looked very much like it was wearing shoes.

Unperturbed by the caterpillar's appearance, Gerald continued to examine the mite. In the magnified image, he looked closely at the shoeless foot, intrigued as to why it was the only one without markings. The miniscule limb was bruised and bleeding. Knowing that the caterpillar was badly hurt and feeling sorry for the insect, Gerald considered what he could do to help. He wasn't sure he was old enough to be responsible for looking after needy things. After all, at only ten years of age, he was the one who was used to being looked after. Being a kind and thoughtful boy though, he contemplated it for a while and then decided that he would do his best to help the creature.

"I'd best get you some help," he said thoughtfully, as he scratted around in his pocket to see what he could use to carry the little chap. He pulled out a fistful of stuff all tangled up in string and placed it on a nearby rock to sort through. Amongst the contents, he had four marbles, chalk, which he used for hopscotch on the back yard, a dirty handkerchief and a penknife. All interesting stuff, he thought, which may have been very useful in any other situation but not this. The hanky could have helped, but it was far too big for a bandage on one so small and he didn't want to risk smothering him.

The caterpillar was so bright that the birds could see him easily and despite Gerald's presence, they still swooped down to try and pick up the tasty-looking morsel. Gerald hated birds; he'd been scared of them ever since he could remember. He disliked the way that they soared and then plummeted on to their prey, it reminded him of the planes which had flown over in the war.

."Get off me tabs," he shouted as he frantically waved his arms at the swooping birds, intent on getting their kill. He scoured through his belongings for a suitable vessel but despite his best efforts, Gerald had nothing to carry him in. Knowing that he needed to get the caterpillar out of danger, he swiftly untangled his penknife from the string and expertly cut the stalk off the leaf on which the caterpillar was sitting. Relieved, Gerald gently lifted the strange-looking insect from his nest in the undergrowth and cradled him protectively in his mud-stained hand; he wanted so desperately to get away from the greedy birds.

"Well I've took you now," he said. "I'll have to help you." Gazing at the tiny creature Gerald wondered where he could find something suitable to carry him in, without being detected. He wracked his young brain for an ideal case. After some thought the perfect vessel popped into his head. "Yes!" he yelped, as he remembered where his Aunty Aggie hid her secret smokes. Carefully, he cupped the caterpillar safely in his left hand, while with his right he quickly grabbed all his other prized possessions. He shoved them back into his pocket, taking extra care not to put them in the one with the big hole. Checking that no one was looking, Gerald tiptoed across the stream, grabbed his shoes and socks and hotfooted it down the hill to his home.

Creeping quietly down the side alley, he sneaked undetected to the bottom of the garden. When he arrived he saw that the outside lavatory door was wide open, so he confidently went inside. Grateful that Aunty Aggie was a little bit sneaky in her pastimes, he reached hopefully behind the pot waste pipe.

"Thanks Anty Aggie," he grinned as he pulled out a half-empty Swan Vesta matchbox. The capsule wasn't perfect; it was a little soggy. "Oh it will have to do for now," he grumbled to himself. Knowing that it was bound to dry out on such a hot day, Gerald steadily emptied the damp box, roughly tore off the edge of the newspaper hanging on the hook next to the lavatory and placed it inside the matchbox to create a bed for the insect. Gently, he put the caterpillar inside and closed the lid, leaving a small gap for air. Wanting to avoid any suspicion, he placed the matchbox safely on the ground while he climbed on to the wooden toilet seat and stretched up to reach his auntie's Woodbine cigarette packet, which was securely hidden from view on top of the cistern. Retrieving the packet successfully, Gerald placed the remaining matches inside the cigarette packet and quickly returned it to its hiding place, ensuring that it was put back exactly where he had found it. Feeling very proud of himself and satisfied that he had done enough to leave the crime undetected, he lifted the matchbox off the floor and vacated the lavatory, leaving the door a little ajar.

Gerald needed a place to think about what he was going to do next and so knowing that the youngest of his brothers Alfie would be out and his grandpa would be at Aunty Aggie's having his weekly haircut, he sped up the garden into his house. Gerald slid in through the back door and up the stairs; he could hear his mum chatting in the front room to his two older sisters, so he knew he wouldn't be disturbed. Checking that the three upstairs bedrooms were completely empty, Gerald entered his overcrowded room. Unlike Alfie, Gerald didn't mind sharing with his grandpa, even though his bad drinking habit made him grumpy and gave him flatulence. The incessant snoring didn't bother him either, because his grandpa could be kind and would often tell stories about his dad when he was a young boy and he'd put up with anything to have the joy of hearing those.

In the sanctuary of his bedroom he began to think about who he could trust with such a secret. Who was wise enough to help him, loving enough to even care and willing enough to believe him? He'd told so many fibs and so often over the last two years, that it was going to be difficult to find someone to believe him.

Opening the box, Gerald sighed as he looked down at the mystical creature gazing back at him. "James and Michael would have loved you," he said, as he thought of his two dear friends back in London. He had no one he could really confide in, as he'd not made any real friends since they'd left, he'd been so close to the two brothers that it made it difficult for anyone to replace them. "Going to have to tell someone about you because I dunt know what to do with you now I've took you," he whispered as he steadily tipped the brightly coloured caterpillar on to the palm of his hand and peered at him.

Gerald's large family unit meant that he was never alone, but he had no one special in his life that he could share his secrets with, being the last child in his mother's brood and a late addition. Gerald was not close to his siblings. He'd tried to be part of the family but his attempts had just left him feeling like he didn't truly belong. He had three brothers and two sisters. Each brother and sister resembled their father in some way or another but Gerald's looks were governed by his mother's side with distinct fair hair and twinkly blue eyes. Ever since he could remember he had always felt like the oddball in the family.

Alfie, at 15, was the nearest to Gerald's age but they weren't friendly. Alfie made Gerald feel like he was a nuisance and would complain bitterly when he wanted to join in with his friends and their games. His two sisters Margaret and Ethel, despite being in their very late teens still lived at home as well. He'd tried to fit in and share their interests, but the age gap was too big for him to have anything really in common with them. The only siblings that had any time for Gerald were his two elder brothers, but both had been called up to do national service, so Gerald very rarely got to see them. Charlie had followed his dad into the RAF and Billy was in the army.

Gerald pondered about who could help him. There was no doubt that it had to be an adult. He recoiled as he remembered times in the past when adults too had shunned him. He felt that most had no time or patience for the things that he felt were important. On his mother's side, Gerald had two aunties which lived close by. Aunty Lily, who was his mother's middle sister, had a massive family, who with the exception of Geoffrey were all girls. He'd been to visit her only a month or so ago but she didn't welcome him with open arms! Despite being a boy amongst so many girls she hadn't even noticed him; she was simply confused as to why the ten cups of tea she had made for her large brood still left one child without a cup.

"Who's here that shunt be?" she'd bellowed. Seeing that she wasn't prepared for any visitors and that she had enough on her plate, Gerald had decided that it was best not to visit for a while. Reflecting back on the scene now, as he sat silently in his room, Gerald realised that his Aunty Lily had been dealing with new-borns every year since she was 25. Two births had produced two sets of twins, so he understood her exhaustion as much as it hurt him.

In stark contrast to his Aunty Lily, his mum's youngest sister Aggie was very fond of Gerald, she had no children and so cherished Gerald like her own. He considered sharing his secret with her but didn't want to put her in a difficult position with his mum. The sisters were particularly close and shared everything. Gerald loved his mum but she'd found him tiresome lately because of his lies and she was unlikely to entertain anything he had to say. He had felt rejected when his friends had returned home and so he couldn't risk feeling any more neglected than he already did by his mother.

"There must be someone that can help me," Gerald whispered to himself, as his mind raced through the adults that he knew. Recollecting the mishaps he had had with his friends during their exploits, he smiled as one man's name came to the forefront of his mind. "Albert." His eyes gleamed as he recalled what a constant he had been in his life for so long. Not only was Albert Armshaw his best friends' uncle, he was his dad's best friend too. Gerald knew that his mother, Florence, had always been fond of Albert, but in her husband's absence they had become closer still. When his nephews had returned home Albert had continued to visit Gerald and his mother for a while, but without the two boys in tow, people began to comment that Albert's frequent visits were inappropriate.

Disturbed by the unkind remarks and suggestions Florence began to sever their friendship and then suddenly one day Albert's visits just stopped altogether. His mother had changed when she became parted from Albert, she grew solemn. Gerald never did understand why Albert had distanced himself from the Hughes family; he saw no reason why he shouldn't spend time with them, he had made his mum so happy and become like a father to him.

Sorrow filled his eyes as he realised that Albert must have had good reason to break away from his family unit. Gerald pictured him alone in his big house, bereft of his nephews and of his adopted family, and bent his head in shame as it dawned on him that he had abandoned Albert too. Willingly Gerald had taken all the love and affection that Albert was prepared to offer him in his dad's absence and yet he had not questioned why he had not come to visit, or even attempted to visit him either. Guiltily he placed the caterpillar back in his matchbox and stored him amongst his things under his bed in his keepsake box out of the way of prying eyes. The evening was fast approaching and Gerald lay back on his bed with his hands interlocked behind his head and decided that tomorrow he would rectify the situation, he'd visit Albert and let him share in this new joy that he'd found.

Day Two

A Friend to Help

The sunshine streamed in through the half-drawn curtains of Gerald's bedroom, holding the promise of yet another glorious summer's day. The heat from the morning sun bore down on to Gerald's face and drowsily he awoke from his deep sleep. As he opened his eyes, he smiled as he remembered his new friend lurking underneath his bed amongst his things. Gerald leapt up quickly and peeked over at the beds adjacent to his own. Their occupants had left. He peeped through his bedroom door on to the landing, making sure that it was also free from his foes. Scrambling on his belly Gerald slid underneath his bedstead in search of his new pet. It didn't take him long to locate the keepsake box, still hidden amongst his most treasured belongings. Reaching inside, Gerald took the delicate matchbox from within and held it gently in his hand. He stopped and listened carefully to make sure that the coast was clear and then shuffled himself backwards from beneath his bed along the dusty bare floorboards out into the open.

Gerald clambered quickly to his feet and climbed back on to his bed. Sitting up tall he pressed his back firmly against the metal bedstead and nervously slid back the lid of the matchbox to find the tiny caterpillar still breathing within.

"Oh thank goodness for that!" he sighed, relieved to see him still safely inside. He'd taken a huge risk leaving him within a stone's throw of Alfie, he thought, as he revelled in the thrill that the caterpillar was just where he'd left him. Gerald looked down at the tiny insect and thought how frail he looked. "HUUUH!" he gasped, as he realised that it hadn't eaten for hours. "You must be starving," he said as he started to panic, cursing himself for not thinking to give him any food. Carefully he placed the caterpillar on his bed, hopped off and hurriedly dressed in yesterday's clothes.

Believing himself suitably attired for another hot summer's day, Gerald scooped up the caterpillar's vessel in his small hand and delicately closed its lid, taking care to leave a small gap for air. Not wanting to cause a scene or arouse any suspicion, Gerald slipped casually down the stairs and walked steadily towards the front door.

Just as he was pulling the door shut, he heard his mother's voice call after him, "Where you off to?"

Gerald poked his head back through the door and called brightly, "Just off to swing, see you later Mam."

"What about some breakfast?" his mother called after him, but Gerald didn't answer he was in too much of a hurry.

Swiftly he made his way up the road and across the fields in search of sustenance for the caterpillar and a long overdue reconciliation with his mum's old friend. Panting heavily after his energetic run and feeling a little warm in his tank top, Gerald dropped down on to the damp ground and welcomed the dampness from the morning's dew. He quickly gathered some blades of grass for his hungry pet, carefully slid back the matchbox lid and placed them inside. Satisfied that his new friend had enough food for his journey, Gerald headed in the direction of Albert's house.

Albert lived in a large house on the other side of town. His residence had been a tad run down when his nephews had first come to stay but he'd made many changes during their lodging and by the time his nephews had returned home to their mother, Albert had turned it into a nice place to live. The walk to Albert's house was a fairly long way for a boy of such short stature and he'd have to walk because he didn't have a farthing to his name. Joyriding on the bus was no longer an option, as the bus driver had warned him that if he caught him on the back of his bus again he'd personally take him to PC Joyce. Gerald shuddered as he thought of the miserable local bobby; he was not at all tolerant of naughty children, so Gerald thought it best to walk. As he walked the long, but familiar route to Albert's house, he was thankful that it wasn't a Sunday, as his mother would have insisted that he wear his best shoes. His Sunday best pair were two sizes too small for him, but his mother said that he had to wear them despite his objections that they actually crippled his toes.

"I'd have had blisters if I'd worn them shoes," he mused as he glanced down at the matchbox stowed carefully in his hand.

After travelling up hill and down dale for over half an hour, Gerald caught sight of Albert's home in the distance. He beamed as he recalled the days he'd spent there in summer's past with his two best friends. Albert had been such fun and his nephews had relished their time with him. Unlike other evacuees, they had been welcomed with open arms when Albert had been asked to take them in. Gerald smiled as he visualised Albert dressed top to toe in his usual bright colours and wondered whether he still chose to wear the same colours as he had when the evacuees had lived with him. Eccentric in nature, Albert didn't mind if the shades didn't coordinate, nor cared if things were worn out or were no longer in fashion, so long as it was in the colour of his choice. Everyone knew that his colour choice was just a phase and it was just a matter of time before he found a new colour to love. He had been equally obsessed with different colours in the past; the tartan phase remained vivid in Gerald's mind.

Keen to see his old friend, Gerald quickened his pace. He felt a little apprehensive as he got closer to the house, but as he approached, his nerves soon disappeared. He began to chuckle when he saw two familiar legs dressed in maroon corduroy trousers, sticking ungainly out from the top of a large wooden container. Laughing affectionately to himself, Gerald coughed lightly to alert Albert to his presence.

"Who's there?" mumbled Albert excitedly from his uncompromising position from inside the box. Carefully Gerald stowed his precious cargo in his pocket and peeped over the top of the box, taking care not to snag his hand-knitted tank top on the loose splinters.

"It's me Albert," he said timidly.

"Gerald?" Albert replied with a surprised, yet warm, tone in his voice. Delighted that Gerald had come to visit Albert clambered to his feet inside the container and smiled a broad smile at his young companion. "Hello, my dear boy how wonderful to see you," he grinned. Seeing the intrigued look in Gerald's eyes, Albert pointed at the mysterious object hidden from view and said, "Would you care to see what it is?"

"Yes please!" Gerald nodded enthusiastically keen to see what was hidden under the large dust sheet.

Without further ado, Albert pulled back the cloth and with a joyous, "Ta-dah!" Albert looked to Gerald for a response. Gerald stared at the contraption in amazement.

"What is it?" Gerald asked.

Albert stood back with his arms wide apart and sighed, "Isn't she just splendid!" Albert had surpassed himself this time. He had successfully managed to merge his two passions, his love of colour and his desire for reckless speed!

After successfully mounting his new toy, Albert expertly thrust down the gas pedal and accelerated out through the unlocked jaws of the container and into the open.

"Woo hoo!" he whooped loudly as he raced his shiny maroon Manx Norton motorcycle gleefully around his dusty field, like he was ten years old himself. His chickens clucked madly and scattered in every direction as he ploughed between them.

Eventually Albert came tootling back to where Gerald had stood patiently waiting. Albert was grinning from ear to ear with joy, his grey windswept comb-over dangling loosely over his left cheek. Albert lovingly parked his new toy, brushed his hair across the top of his head with the palm of his hand and made his way towards Gerald.

"It is so lovely to see you Gerald and on such a momentous day as this as well," he announced enthusiastically. Thrilled with Albert's response Gerald dashed towards his estranged friend and hugged him tightly.

"I've really missed you Albert," Gerald whimpered.

Albert returned his young companion's grasp with a fatherly squeeze, ruffled his short blonde hair and said, "My dear boy I can't begin to express how much I have missed all of you," his eyes glazing over with tears.

Contented that nothing had changed between them, Albert turned to Gerald and asked, "So what do you think of my new bike, young man?" Gerald laughed at the comical contraption standing awkwardly outside Albert's home.

"She's right nice," Gerald agreed and after several more minutes of admiring his bike and explaining all the technical gismos that it had on it, Albert was satisfied that Gerald was as enamoured with the new motorbike as he was.

Looking down at his weary young friend, he smiled and after pulling him into a fatherly embrace he said, "Let us get you something to eat shall we?" Tired and peckish from his journey, Gerald welcomed Albert's affection and raced inside his house for nourishment. He was anxious to reveal his new pet but knew that Albert would not be happy until his guest had consumed enough to quench both his hunger and his thirst. Gerald ate hungrily and after two cups of tea, a rather large slice of fruit cake and six ginger biscuits, Gerald felt brave enough to show Albert his discovery.

Unsure whether Albert would believe his story, Gerald thought it best to just show him the caterpillar rather than trying to explain. Taking the creature out of his pocket, Gerald presented Albert with the small matchbox.

"What's this, I do hope you have not taken up smoking Gerald?" Albert said, staring down at the Swan Vesta box in his hand.

"No, no," Gerald giggled. "Nowt like that." He reached across and slid open the lid. Albert looked curiously at Gerald and then took the small container in his hand to examine its contents.

"Oh he is really quite beautiful Gerald, wherever did you find him?" Albert exclaimed enthusiastically. Gerald explained what had happened and Albert stroked his chin thoughtfully.

Still pondering, Albert casually walked across to his coatrack, took down his tasselled cap and placed it firmly on his head, taking care to tuck in all his loose strands of hair.

"Near to the tree swing, you say?" Albert said sceptically.

"Yes just over tuther side of stream!" Gerald replied in a certain tone. Albert mused over this affirmation and questioned to himself how it was at all possible for the creature to be discovered in the north Nottinghamshire countryside when it looked so rare.

Carefully, Albert removed the caterpillar from the matchbox and placed it on a tin tray which he'd found randomly on the floor. Gerald swiftly took his magnifying glass out of his pocket and handed it to Albert.

"Do you want to lend me magnifying glass Albert to take proper look at him?" Graciously, Albert accepted the trusty magnifying glass from Gerald's grasp and took a closer look. On further examination Albert spotted the damaged foot and black markings around his eyes.

"Do you know I think we should name him Douglas," Albert said laughing lightly to himself as he peered at the tiny creature.

"Douglas? Why Douglas?" Gerald replied.

"Are you not aware of the famous pilot Douglas Bader? He of course lost both of his legs in the war," Albert mused to himself. "Here boy take a closer look at his markings. Do you not think he resembles a pilot?" Gerald changed places with Albert and peered through the magnified image at the tiny creature. "See," Albert pointed out. "Here around his eyes. Does it not look like he's wearing goggles, to you?"

"Oh I get it now, yeh he does dunt he!" Gerald agreed enthusiastically.

"Come on, let's see what we can do for the little chap," Albert said kindly, as he placed his arm affectionately around Gerald's shoulders. The duo swiftly moved through the house and terminated in a small room at the very far end, which Gerald had never seen before. Albert was a keen amateur scientist it seemed, from the numerous dusty jars with various potions strewn around inside. The shelved walls were donned with endless books and other unmentionables dangled from the wooden beams. Gerald looked on in amazement as he took in his surroundings, feeling an overwhelming sense of achievement in choosing this clever individual to help him. Albert carefully put Douglas on his workbench and took off his maroon velvet smoking jacket placing it tidily on the hook behind him. He pulled open the glass door of an old cabinet on the wall and took out a small tin box and empty jam jar. Placing the tin box on the table he ventured into a tiny kitchen which housed a sink and filled the jam jar with water before returning to the workbench.

Leisurely he pulled up a chair and beckoned Gerald to his side. "Be so kind as to hold this over him would you, there's a good chap," he said, as he handed him back his magnifying glass. Dutifully Gerald did as he was told and Albert set to work. Prudently he cleaned the excess blood from around Douglas' sore foot with the edge of his own handkerchief which he'd dipped into the fresh water. Gerald watched as Albert meticulously cleared the blood away from the tiny insect's foot and then tamed further bleeding with tiny strips of gauze which he had taken from the tin box. Content that he had done all he could, Albert pushed the magnifying glass aside and stood up. Turning to face Gerald he sighed, "I'm afraid that's all I can do for him for now, Gerald." Seeing that Gerald had concern in his eyes, Albert bent down to his young companion and looked him confidently in his blue eyes. "Come, come now, time's a great healer you know!" he said as he patted him on his arm. "Let's see what we can find out about the little fellow, shall we young man?" Albert said, feeling that further investigation was needed. Albert rummaged through his vast library of encyclopaedias in an attempt to classify the caterpillar and passed Gerald a book on insect habitat and general diet. "I think he must be frightfully rare though,

Gerald," Albert mumbled as he disappointingly flicked through his book on breeds. He was a clever man, who many had coined as 'The fountain of all knowledge' but Gerald was sure that even he was stumped on this occasion.

After hours of reading and researching about the better striped breeds, Gerald's tummy began to gurgle at first and then rumbled loudly, alerting him to both the need for food and his fast approaching teatime.

Albert laughed knowingly and said, "Golly it has just occurred to me that I myself have had no nourishment since breakfast either." They both agreed that they should partake in a morsel of some sort or another.

Despite living by himself Albert always ate heartily and he was a very good cook. Earlier that day alongside the cake that Gerald had sampled when he had first arrived, he had prepared a cottage loaf. The aroma of the delicious freshly baked bread tantalised Gerald's taste buds.

Albert laughed loudly as he heard Gerald's tummy rumble again, he winked and asked, "Would you like to try some of this excellent bread and dripping? I do believe it would most certainly rid you of those hunger pangs and it is rather super too."

"Oh yeh please, that'd be lovely," Gerald replied as his empty belly growled yet again in anticipation. Gerald's mouth filled with water and he licked his lips as he watched Albert slice the soft warm white bread into thick rounds and spread the smooth white dripping on generously, so that it melted magnificently into the dough. Gratefully Gerald took the wedge from Albert's fingers and sunk his teeth into the delicious snack. "Mmm," he said contentedly.

"Come along young man," Albert said as he motioned Gerald towards outside. "I see no reason why we should stand on ceremony," he declared as they made their way into the open and took up residence on the garden bench to devour their tea. Gerald was in heaven, as he swung his legs back and forth savouring the wedge, which Albert had expertly seasoned with salt and pepper, which made all the difference.

After consuming the rest of his bread and dripping, Albert raised his glass of beer. "You know that on special occasions it is customary to make a toast and today of all days certainly warrants an appropriate toast, do you not concur Gerald?" Gerald nodded in agreement. "Would you care to do the honours, or should I?"

"I can't think of nowt to say Albert so you'd best do it." Albert chinked Gerald's bottle of Tizer and smiled brightly at his young companion.

"To the rekindling of old friendships and finding new ones," Albert cheered.

Delighted that Douglas had been included in the toast Gerald lifted his drink and gaily chinked Albert's brimming drink, "To Douglas."

The rest of the day passed quickly and Gerald stayed well into the early evening before deciding it was time to return home. It was decided that Albert should keep Douglas overnight, as he had the right provisions to feed him and a safe place for him to stay. They agreed that they would meet at the town library in the morning to see if they could find out any more about Douglas. Despite the little information that they had gained about the caterpillar, Gerald felt elated, he'd had a wonderful day, perhaps the best he'd ever had. Confident that his charge was in the safe hands of his eccentric friend and happy that he had rekindled a friendship that he thought he'd lost, Gerald said his goodbyes and stepped off the porch and headed in the direction of home.

"Bye," he called as he turned to wave at his two friends lingering on the porch. Smiling and feeling pleased with himself he swung his leg round to mount his imaginary horse, pulled tight on the reins and slapped his bottom yelling, "Yee–hah!" at the top of his voice. He galloped energetically home with joy in his heart, he was a true hero on horseback and he was going to ride like the wind.

Day Three
The Magic Begins

Bright and early in the morning Gerald awoke ravenous, his mother had been so upset and worried when he'd come in so late, that she sent him straight to bed without any supper. With his empty belly aching for food, he washed and dressed and hurriedly made his way downstairs in search of nourishment. As he descended the bare staircase, he could hear the musical sound of a song he knew coming from the wireless. Putting his hands together, he looked up to the ceiling and prayed that a bit of Glenn Miller's '*In the mood*' had mellowed his mother's temper from the night before.

Walking uneasily into the kitchen, he inhaled a deep breath and approached his mother. "Morning Mam," Gerald said brightly as he caressed her fair soft skin with a gentle kiss. His mother, Florence, lifted her head up from her ironing and looked him discerningly in the eye as he took his usual place at the breakfast table.

"Morning Gerald," she replied sternly with an obvious annoyance still trickling through her veins. Gerald smiled meekly back at his mother, knowing that she was bound to have further questions. "So where'd you get to last night? I were worried sick," Florence probed. Defensively Gerald pulled his chair up tightly to the table and swallowed hard.

"I were with Albert, Mam," he said timidly.

Florence stared at Gerald, momentarily she said nothing and then she thoughtfully placed her iron to one side on the hob to reheat. Slowly she walked from behind her ironing board to join Gerald at the table and pulled out a kitchen chair. She slid on to the wooden seat opposite Gerald and reached for her cup, before drawing her chair in close. She tilted her head to one side and cradled her lukewarm tea reflectively in her hands.

"How is me old friend?" she asked. Gerald stared at his mother in disbelief for her reaction was not what he had expected. She'd been so angry the previous night, that he hadn't relished telling her where he'd been. Florence's eyes glistened as her youngest child relayed the story of Albert on his new bike. She flushed as he described his new maroon attire and she listened intently as he told her about the delicious food he had prepared and the fun they'd had.

"Sounds like you was in safe hands," Florence said approvingly as she stood to continue her chores. To Gerald's relief his mother didn't probe for any further explanation, she was satisfied that he had been with her dear friend and that was enough for her. Gerald devoured his breakfast while he observed his mother as she worked. He watched her intently as she reached to take another hot iron off the hob; expertly grasping the wrought-iron handle with the moleskin cloth. She turned it over and quickly spat on it to test that it was hot enough to use. Vigorously she pushed and pulled the heavy hobbin' iron back and forth across the wide board. Gerald watched his mother as she methodically folded and sorted the starched items into their owner's piles. She had loving hands, he thought as he witnessed them work, her fingers were smooth and plump but Gerald grinned as he recalled how she could magically stroke the ache out of any sore foot.

Catching his gaze, her blue, almost tearful eyes, met his and her lips curled upwards in a loving response. Gerald wished he could see deep within the blue lagoons, as they held a secret that he couldn't reach and a sadness which he didn't understand. Despite her firmness, Gerald knew that his mum loved him and he echoed her silent admission of it with a small smile of his own. His bowl empty after his welcomed breakfast, he sat back in his chair and glanced around the room. On the mantelshelf above the fireplace he stared at the old photographs all proudly framed. Amongst the collection of family pictures there was a photograph of his mum taken years before as a youngster. She'd been lovely, he thought, a real beauty. In the old picture she had a glow about her which he didn't recognise. He looked at his mother, now in her forties, her hair pulled purposely back in a low practical bun and he wondered when the radiant glow had disappeared.

Next to the picture of the young Florence was a wedding photograph, Gerald turned and glanced lovingly at his mother. He wondered if the absence of her husband had drained the life out of her, causing her to age prematurely. Returning his gaze to the shelf, his eyes came to rest on the standard issue uniformed pose of his father. The war had taken many casualties, amongst them were sons, brothers and fathers, Gerald's dad had been one of them. He'd never known his father; he'd only been a toddler when his mother opened the yellow telegram from the War Office. Her husband was missing in action, presumed dead and all she could do was wait in the hope that one day he'd be found and come home to her. Gerald looked at his mum and contemplated what it must be like not knowing if her husband was alive or dead. Sympathetically he considered how difficult that must have been to deal with over the last seven years and began to understand her lack of lust for life.

"You alright lad?" his mum asked, looking at his serious face.

"Yeh I'm OK," Gerald replied as he gulped back the tears welling up in his eyes. He knew so very little about his dad, he thought sadly, the stories that his grandpa told him kept his memory alive but there was so little to remember him by. Safely stowed away under his bed he kept the only things he had of his dad's; some small hand-carved wooden toys, which his grandpa had given him and a photograph of his dad holding him as a small child before he left for war. Grandpa had been a carpenter in his younger days and Gerald's dad had obviously inherited his skill. On his sixth birthday, he'd been delighted to receive the wooden toys. He had listened keenly as his grandpa described how his dad had sculptured them with such skill and intricate detail and Gerald had marvelled at his dad's craftsmanship. Pleased that he'd been given such a wonderful gift and touched that his grandpa had chosen him above all his other siblings to have the wooden toys, he'd treasured them ever since.

"So what you up to today, then ducky?" Gerald's mum said cheerily, breaking his trance. Quickly he looked up at his mother and instantly began to fret, he wanted so desperately to tell his mum all about Douglas, but he didn't want to risk upsetting her when her good mood had only just been restored. Gerald had such a vivid imagination and his elaborate stories had fooled the most gullible of his relatives on numerous occasions, but this wasn't something she would believe without proof and he wasn't ready to share his secret with her yet.

"Albert's taken me to library," he said honestly.

His mother cocked her head to one side and pursed her lips. "Really!" she said suspiciously.

"Yes, honestly Mam," he said. "He said we was going to look at some pictures of them bikes he likes," he replied convincingly. He had lied so often in the past, that his answer rolled credibly off his tongue and thankfully his mother was convinced.

"I bet you'll fair enjoy that sweetheart," she beamed. "Better not be too late this time, though eh!" she warned as she collected the ironed clothes and made her ascent up the stairs. Gathering up his breakfast dishes he took them dutifully over to the big Belfast sink. He washed and rinsed them through and left them to dry on the wooden draining board. Reluctant to do any more chores and conscious that he only had a short while before he met Albert, he made haste out of the front door, keen to continue with the next instalment of his adventure. As he ran down his road and headed into the town, he thought about Douglas. Although he was only ten, he understood that he was no ordinary caterpillar; he knew he must be special as he'd certainly never seen an insect with such markings before. He wondered how Douglas had been overnight, but was sure that Albert had taken great care of him.

Approaching the library entrance, Gerald spotted Albert's familiar figure waiting as prompt and as brightly dressed as ever. Dressed in grey knee-length socks, maroon check plus fours and matching argyle tank top, he beamed as he saw Gerald approaching.

"You look smart," Gerald commented as he admired his friend's outfit.

"Oh thank you Gerald that's very kind of you to say so. I do believe that special occasions require flawless outfits," he beamed as he removed his smoking pipe from his mouth. Looking left and then right and satisfied that no one was in earshot of his words, Albert bent down to

Gerald and quietly whispered in his ear. "You really will not believe the transformation in Douglas... He looks really quite magnificent now!"

Eager to see the change in Douglas, Gerald raced to get inside. He had passed the library many times before when he came to town with his mother, but they never went inside. It was a beautiful old building which had fortunately survived the war unscathed. As Gerald entered the room he was taken in by its aroma, a subtle hint of leather and years of accumulated dust. The tired dark green carpet was threadbare; the dark wooden bookshelves lining the aisles stretched up high and heaved with books. Gerald's mouth gaped open as he tiptoed quietly through the impressive room towards the information desk. He'd never seen such a place.

Unsure of where to start looking, the friends approached the information desk and from behind the counter emerged a rather plump lady in her mid-forties. She wore her dark brown hair in the latest fashion and was immaculately dressed in an undersized black dress. She had a small spotted scarf tied neatly in a bow around her neck and dark-rimmed glasses perched on the end of her rather pointed nose. She was an attractive lady and Albert acknowledged that by smiling brightly at her. The lady returned his gesture with a bright, but false smile.

"Morning gentlemen how may I help?" she purred as she leaned up against the desk.

Her name was Mrs Lesley Osbourne and she was a very nosey individual. Despite only living in the village for just over two years, she had made it her business to know everyone else's. Although she was overly friendly to those she met, she was not a nice woman and yet everyone fell for her charms. She was so subtle in her approach that before you knew it you'd divulged your deepest darkest secrets and not realised until it was too late. Gerald had recognised her instantly; she had befriended his mum for a while. They had become firm friends when she'd arrived in the village and they'd spent hours at the kitchen table laughing and joking.

Lesley was a war widow and Florence had felt an instant connection with her in the absence of her own husband. She did all she could to make her feel welcome and included her new friend in everything. Lesley became a big part of the family, but their friendship quickly waned when Lesley met her new husband and saw no need for Florence's friendship. They made polite conversation when their paths crossed but gradually Florence pulled away altogether. She'd never had a friendship so intense before and she felt betrayed and let down. Gerald studied the plump lady behind the counter as she chatted away to Albert and considered how cruel she'd been to his mum. Florence was bereft of her husband and her best friend whom she had trusted and treasured had abandoned her for the same thing that she had lost. Anger rose in his blood as she stood before him and he understood why his mother always quickened their pace now as they passed the library doors.

Mrs Oh-so Nosey! As Gerald had heard his mum refer to her, advised Albert where he needed to go to find the encyclopaedias and reference section and then turned her attention to Gerald. Rubbing his blonde hair and squeezing his cheeks she greeted Gerald with affection.

"Hello Gerald, gosh you've grown. How's your mum? Haven't seen her for ages!" she enquired in a genuine tone. "Any news about your dad? So sad isn't it!" she nodded in agreement with herself as she looked pensively at Albert.

"We really should be getting on now Lesley," Albert interrupted kindly as he saw the signs of inquisitiveness building in the conversation.

"Oh OK Albert no problem, no problem at all, if you are sure you don't need any further assistance," she called disappointedly, as he quickly terminated the conversation.

"Yes quite sure my dear. I think that we will be fine to navigate ourselves in the right direction now, thanks for your help," he called as he swiftly steered Gerald away from the wretched woman. True to form she had intended to get as much information out of the little boy as she could muster. Albert was aware of how hurt Florence had been and he was determined not to let this despicable lady learn anything about his old friend's life. On occasions when Gerald had seen her in the past he'd been guarded as his mother had instructed him to be. Today he was like a closed book as he had a secret to protect and wasn't going to divulge anything.

Patting his young friend's shoulder he said, "I do believe it's this way Gerald," and they walked nonchalantly towards the far end of the library. Unconcerned whether the librarian was out of earshot or not Albert turned to Gerald and impulsively said, "She can't help being nosey you know, I just think she's a very lonely woman."

"What do you mean Albert?" Gerald replied.

"Well I know that she appears to have everything," Albert began.

"Yeh like a big house and loads of money!" Gerald interrupted.

"Yes, I can see why you'd think that, but appearances can be deceptive you know and sometimes things aren't always as they seem," Albert said raising his eyebrows.

"If she were so lonely, why dint she want to be mates with me Mam then Albert?" Gerald asked thoughtfully.

"Well I can't be certain but if I were to hazard a guess I would say that she saw what your mum had and couldn't contain her jealously and eventually it got in the way of their friendship," Albert replied.

"You mean she's got no family like me Mam don't you Albert?" Gerald said.

"Yes Gerald you have to feel sorry for her really. I understand she lost her own mother when she was very young, which must have made it difficult for her to build loving relationships."

"I suppose not being able to have children of her own must have been really hard to accept an all," Gerald said as he turned to glance back at Lesley. He watched as she revelled in her own self-importance from behind her counter absorbing herself in other people's business and thriving on the acquisition of gossip.

Part of him understood why Lesley chose to live life the way she did. He knew all too well what it felt like to lose the ones you love and feel alone. For the first time he saw what a shallow life she lead with the absence of real meaning and he felt sorry for her. His mum had offered her true friendship and she had rejected it. Gerald too had tried to avoid hurt by isolating himself from the ones he loved and he realised that he didn't want to end up like her. He was glad that Lesley was no longer his mother's friend, she deserved better and he hoped that her resentment would melt away in time, leaving nothing but pure pity for the cold-hearted woman.

The twosome walked along the tall thin corridors and located a booth out of sight of prying eyes. Carefully Albert pulled down his knapsack from his shoulder, placing it gently on the wooden bench. Leaving Gerald seated at the worktop, Albert returned to the reference section and searched inquisitively along the shelves for books on rare breeds. Slowly Gerald pulled the bag towards him and reached within. Discreetly swishing his hand around inside, Gerald searched for the small matchbox.

"Dear boy you won't find the matchbox in there," Albert chirruped as he sat down opposite Gerald, his arms overloaded with books.

"Where is he then?" Gerald said anxiously.

"Don't concern yourself Gerald. I didn't say he wasn't in there," Albert replied reassuringly as he reached inside the bag, "I simply remarked that you wouldn't find the matchbox in there. You see I had to discard it, it was no longer adequate for Douglas' needs." Albert smiled proudly as he pulled Douglas out of the bag to reveal his recent transformation. Douglas had grown! He was now the size of a small slug. Douglas' carriage had been upgraded to a jam jar. A piece of greaseproof paper was on the top which had been pricked with air holes and secured with an elastic band. Albert had provided him with green leaves to munch on and a short thick twig to crawl up and down.

"Wow," Gerald gasped as he stared at Douglas' feet, he was big enough now that you could see him clearly without the magnifying glass. Gerald couldn't believe his eyes, no longer were there markings on each foot. They had been transformed, as if by magic, into magnificent shoes.

"Just like Fred Astaire's shiny dancing shoes, wouldn't you agree?" Albert beamed as he pointed to Douglas' feet. The caterpillar's bright green eyes shone through the dark rings around them which still looked like goggles, his wounds were healing and he looked well.

"He's proper magical isn't he Albert?" Gerald said, as he lifted the jar to his face to take a better look.

Despite himself, Albert had to agree and nodded as he whispered, "Yes I agree he really is quite wonderful."

Gerald turned the glass jar around in his fingers to examine the creature in all his glory and caressed the outside of the glass, he was enamoured by the caterpillar. Peering closely through the glass jar Gerald smiled lovingly at him and to his great surprise Douglas smiled back.

"Albert! Did you see that?" he whispered, as he turned to face his friend, but Albert had missed it. He had been so keen to find a logical explanation for it all he had buried his head in the literature he had found and become distracted.

"Mmm...? See what?" Albert replied as he half listened to Gerald's question.

Unsure whether he had imagined it, Gerald said nothing more, so he just smiled and said, "Oh nowt."

"Very well, if you are sure," Albert replied in a dismissive tone and returned to his informative book.

Thoughtfully, Gerald reflected about what had just occurred. Had it been his imagination? Or had he really shown a human-like emotion and smiled at him? He'd wished so hard for something mystical to happen and his eyes twinkled with excitement at the prospect that it could be true. Carefully he stowed Douglas away in Albert's bag. Right from the start, Gerald had felt a connection with the caterpillar and now he knew he was special. He questioned why he was here, why had it been him that found him and why so near to his home? Turning his head slowly he peeked out of his booth and down towards the main desk. They needed to get out of there as quickly as possible, he thought, with such a gossip in the vicinity Douglas could be in real danger. If he really was magical, everyone would want to see him and Gerald wasn't going to let that happen.

After hours at the library, despite Gerald's insistence that they should not stay for long, Albert's research hadn't come to much. Despite his desire for colour in his life, Albert was not a creative or imaginative man; he saw things very much in facts and figures. He'd made his initial assessment of Douglas by his markings and colouring, but trying to substantiate a reason why Douglas was wearing shoes and goggles was proving to be virtually impossible. Albert had to admit that it was rather surreal but it was happening nonetheless and science had been proved wrong in the past, so why not now.

"Come on young man, we had better hurry you home to your mother," Albert said despondently, as he closed the last book on his pile. Gerald protectively scooped up the knapsack and together they made their way out of the library. The two colluded that it was best that Albert took Douglas home with him again, as he was getting too big to hide now, but one thing was for sure they'd have to tell his mum something otherwise she'd worry and Gerald didn't want to upset her.

As the pair reached the terraced steps of Gerald's home, Gerald slipped the knapsack reluctantly off his shoulder and passed it to Albert.

"Don't worry I'll take good care of him for you, you know Gerald," affirmed Albert.

Gerald nodded tearfully, "I know you will. Come in Albert, I'll go fetch me Mam, I'll not be a minute." Confident that he could reassure Florence that her son was in safe hands, Albert followed Gerald into the house in which he had once been so at ease in.

"Hello Florrie," he beamed as he saw her standing by the oven.

"Albert," she said frantically removing her soiled apron and moved quickly to stand protectively behind the kitchen table. "What do I owe this pleasure?" she said stretching her words as she spoke. Albert, seeing her obvious discomfort, pulled out a chair and plonked himself casually at the table.

"It's been far too long has it not Florrie?" he said as he shone her a bright smile. Softened by his relaxed approach, Florence tapped the back of her chair and laughed.

"Suppose you'll be wanting to stay for your tea?"

"What culinary feast is on the menu tonight, Florrie?" Albert said still smiling flirtatiously at her.

"As it happens, its corned beef hash, which I know is your favourite Albert," Florence said giggling girlishly in spite of herself.

"I did think it might be," he winked, as if their friendship had never been broken.

Gerald stood back in awe as he watched Albert's charms transform his mother to a glimmer of her former self. His mother's eyes filled with tears of joy and sadness as they reminisced for hours, first over numerous cups of tea and later over dinner. Convincingly, Albert told Florrie that Gerald would be visiting him for a while to help him look after an injured animal he'd found. Impressed with his fabrication of the truth, Gerald also found himself mesmerised by Albert's persuasive manner. After his tasty meal, Albert insisted on helping with the dishes, and not wanting to outstay his welcome soon bid his farewell to Florence.

Gerald walked Albert to the door. "Thank you," he said.

Albert thinking that he was referring to Douglas rubbed the top of Gerald's blonde hair and said, "My dear boy you have no need to thank me, it was a pleasure."

"No," Gerald replied, as he glanced towards the kitchen. "I meant thank you for making me Mam smile."

Albert pursed his lips together and sighed, "Well Gerald, for that I need no gratitude for the pleasure was all mine," he said as he gently squeezed the side of his young friend's arm. With tears in his eyes, Albert turned on his heel and sauntered away.

"I'll come and see you tomorrow then," Gerald shouted a little bemused by Albert's comments. Albert lifted his hand in the air in acknowledgement and continued on his journey.

Returning to the kitchen Gerald watched his mother as she moved elegantly around the room, he'd never seen her so happy. He looked up at the photograph of his mother that he'd studied earlier that day and for the first time he saw the glow in the portrait now upon the smiling face of his mother. He knew that Albert had set her mind at ease and left assuring her he'd take good care of her boy, but Gerald could see that his visit had given her more than just reassurance. Albert had completely captivated his mum; he couldn't believe the transformation in her character. He'd never noticed what his mother had been like when Albert had visited her frequently in the past, he'd been too young and preoccupied with his own life to notice. Gerald listened as he heard his mother's sweet voice trill over the top of the music coming from the wireless, a beautiful sound that he realised had been absent from their home for far too long.

Day Four

The Arrival of the Cousins

Gerald had slept late on the Thursday morning and when he awoke the room was empty, below stairs he could hear raucous laughter and the high-pitched voices of children. Knowing instantly who it was in his house, Gerald raced down the stairs three at a time and bounded into the kitchen. Every summer, Gerald's cousins travelled across from Rugeley in Staffordshire and came to stay for two weeks. For a small while his already cramped house heaved gloriously with small children. The Challenders were great fun. Gerald treasured their visits, as his solitary pastimes could be put on hold and he'd have an abundance of friends to play with. Aunty Eileen and Gerald's mum had been best friends at school and then his mum had secured their friendship forever by marrying Eileen's brother, Charlie Hughes.

Eileen had had lots of boyfriends before she met her husband and was even engaged at one point to a local boy; in fact it was while she was on a date with him at the policeman's ball that she met her husband Vic Challender. The whole affair had left the lad heartbroken, he never married, never moved on and still lived in the same house that they had planned to set up home in. He had become bitterer as the years passed, which wasn't a good trait for the local bobby. The cousins had a very different life from Gerald and his family; they were fairly wealthy and fortunate. Their dad was both a retired sergeant in the police force and with the help of his mother a proud publican. The Challender family had numerous perks during the war because of their dad's profession and now that he had bought the lucrative Swan and Partridge outright, all profits were his. Vic never joined his family on their trips to Nottinghamshire; Florence never questioned why, she just supposed that he had to stay at home because of work commitments.

"Eh up me duck," Aunty Eileen chirruped mimicking her long-forgotten Midlands accent. "Did you forget we was coming?" she laughed as she embraced Gerald tightly.

"Yeh I forgot it were Thursday today," Gerald said as he relished her affection.

"Gerald!" Susan screamed excitedly as she ran at full pelt towards her sleepy cousin.

"Hello Suze," he said as he hugged her awkwardly. Susan was the eldest of the three cousins at 13; she was a beautiful confident young lady with long blonde hair, fair skin and the most amazing electric blue eyes. Gerald enjoyed Susan's company the most, as she was extremely clever. He learnt something new from her every time she came to stay. For such a young girl she was a fountain of knowledge, but despite all her qualities and achievements Susan was a pleasant, down-to-earth child who happily fitted in wherever she was placed.

"What about me? Don't I get a hug?" A little voice screeched above all the others. Gerald turned to his side and glanced down. There beside him with her shoulders hunched up towards her little neck, her arms folded tightly and her brow deeply furrowed stood little Josie.

"Ah Jose dint see you there, come and give us a big hug then," he smiled.

"Yeh!" she whooped as she grinned a toothless grin at her big cousin.

"Oh you've lost tooth," Gerald said affectionately as he tapped his own tooth in acknowledgement.

"Yes, Daddy yanked it out!" she said as she winced at the thought.

"Ooh with cotton?" Gerald replied.

"Yes, he tied it to the kitchen door handle and then slammed it shut and out it popped," she said as she re-enacted the door slamming.

"Have you got it?" Gerald asked. Josie rummaged in her knickers' pocket and she gleefully pulled out her lace hanky. The handkerchief was all covered in blood and at one end tightly twisted and neatly encased was a tiny lump. Gerald smiled as he watched the little girl carefully unravel the hanky and proudly thrust the tooth under his nose.

"Dad says he's going to give me a penny for being so brave," she bragged innocently.

"Crikey you're lucky!" Gerald replied, truly believing that she was.

"Say hello to your cousin, Clive," Eileen said sharply as she pulled her son's tank top to get his attention.

"Hello Gerald," he mimicked not taking kindly to being told what to do. Clive was the closest to Gerald's age at 12, but he was very different; he was a wayward child who was always up to mischief. Despite the bigger age gap, it was always Alfie who Clive chose to be as thick as thieves with when he came to stay; Gerald often felt left out from the boys' brigade.

"What you got there, Clive?" Gerald said enthusiastically, trying to get off on a better foot this year. Clive looked Gerald menacingly in his eyes.

"What's it got to do with you?" he sneered, as he cradled the long brown paper package in his arms. Gerald bowed his head, he longed to be part of their gang but despite his pleading he was not allowed to join in with their secret plans.

The fact was, he was not like his cousin and brother; he was prone to telling lies but he was not a naughty boy. Secretly envious of their friendship, Gerald watched the pair whisper and snigger between themselves and wondered what tricks they'd get up to this summer. On his last visit, Clive had told both his cousins that he'd built a small toy garage for the sole purpose of capturing and incarcerating bees. As Gerald's reaction had been one of horror the two elder boys concluded that he wouldn't approve of their mischief so didn't include him in their plans. Gerald had witnessed and stood in awe at the two reprobates as they caused undetected chaos each and every year and wondered if this year he'd have any part in it.

"I've put Clive in with boys, Eileen," Florence said as she guided Clive out of the room, towards the stairs. "But we'll have to juggle sleeping arrangements again next Tuesday when older lads come home."

"Oh that's nice, been a while since I've seen Billy and Charlie," Eileen trilled, as she picked up the girls' cases. "Are my girls doubling up with you two?" she asked as Margaret and Ethel walked into the room.

"Yeh and you're in with me Mam as usual," Margaret replied as she helped her aunty carry her bags.

"Where's Grandpa going Mam?" Ethel asked.

"To your Anty Aggie's for his annual holiday," she replied.

Keen to see what was in the package and aware that he was still in his bed clothes, Gerald subtly vacated the kitchen and quietly followed the cousins up the stairs. Eavesdropping at the closed bedroom door, Gerald could here Alfie's delight as Clive unwrapped the package.

"Are you going use it today Clive?" Alfie asked keenly.

"No, the timing has to be perfect," Gerald heard Clive reply. "If I'm going to get my own back on Johnson, it has to be done properly."

Clive was a mischievous little boy, who had a passion for stealing. Like a magpie he was drawn to shiny things and Gerald had often found other people's belongings hidden in his room, which Clive had taken during his summer vacation. He didn't understand why his cousin stole, as he was quite fortunate, but supposed that it was the thrill of doing it undetected that made it all the more exciting. Gerald listened closely as Clive unfolded his plan to Alfie.

"You're taking a big risk, messing with Sydney Johnson again Clive," said Alfie in a concerned voice.

"Oh I have it all planned out, Alfie you'll see," Clive said confidently.

Gerald pulled back from the door and felt concern for his cousin. Fearing what might happen to Clive this time if he got into trouble, he recalled last summer when old man Johnson had taken drastic near fatal action. Clive was unkind to him, but he'd never hurt him. Sydney Johnson on the other hand was a terrible bully and he didn't wish his cousin to be treated like he had been the previous year. Gerald promised himself that he would do what he could to help him.

Despite his distaste for fruit, Clive enjoyed scrumping and every summer he set about stealing from a different garden. For years he'd got away with it, but last year he met his match. As Clive scrambled on his belly collecting the gooseberries from old man Johnson's orchard, Sydney had unexpectedly woken from his drunken slumber, took out his gun and shot at him. Clive had been so scared that he'd cried like a baby and in his panic got tangled in the fencing just like Peter Rabbit. Johnson who was a big burly man, had lifted the skinny young boy up by his shirt collar and hooked him up high on the scarecrow in his orchard. Pinning a large notice on the front with SCAREDY-CROW written in black paint, he'd left the child to hang out to dry.

Clive had to be rescued once again by Aunty Eileen. She'd secured Clive's release on the promise she'd never let it happen again and to soften the blow, had pledged a keg of ale from their pub on her next visit. Clive had been thankful for the first time that there was only two days of summer left before he could go home. The teasing had been unbearable and he had been really humiliated. The boy was so angry that his loathing grew more and more over the autumn and winter months and by spring he had devised a plan to get his revenge.

Gerald listened closely as Clive explained to Alfie his determination to be king of the scrumpers once again.

"I've got a reputation to get back," he crowed.

"What you going do about Johnson though?" Alfie asked concerned for his cousin.

Clive's voice seethed with anger. "I'm going to make his life a misery."

"How?" Alfie asked.

Clive laughed a sharp dry laugh, "By upsetting his wife, Lorna Johnson." Old man Johnson, despite being of huge stature, was unquestionably browbeaten by his wife. In complete contrast to her husband, Mrs Johnson was a tiny lady both in frame and height. She stood no taller than 4ft 10 inches and weighed less than 7 stone. She was a fierce woman who Adolf Hitler himself wouldn't have messed with. Clive had noted that Mrs Johnson was particularly fond of baking and that her apple pie had won a prize in the village fete every year for the past ten years, this made her very happy indeed. Subsequently old man Johnson was happy when his wife was happy. Since that awful day in the summer, Clive had plotted his revenge and he'd used every spare moment he had to devise and construct a machine so slick that it could reach into the branches of an apple tree and strip Mrs Johnson's apple supply without detection.

"Aren't you getting dressed today Gerald?" Ethel screeched, as she emerged from her overcrowded room. Gerald jolted away from the door.

"Yeh just come up to do that now." On hearing the commotion, Alfie flung open the bedroom door.

"You can't come in yet," he smirked as he guarded the threshold.

"It's OK Alf, let him in," Clive scoffed, confident that his possession was out of sight. Under the watchful eye of his elder siblings, Gerald timidly entered the room and quickly set about getting dressed ready for the day. When he was done, the three boys made haste down the stairs.

"Come on Suze, come on Josie let's go to the fields," Clive called as they reached the bottom step. Thrilled at the prospect, the cousins raced out of the door and up into the fields near Gerald's home. Despite their differences, there were times when they all played happily together and enjoyed the glorious long summer days away from school.

Gerald raced alongside his cousins, joyful that he had them to stay for a while.

"What shall we play?" Josie shouted excitedly.

"What about tick off ground?" Susan chimed.

"No let's play bulldog," Clive called, already swinging from the branch of a tree.

"What about sound your holler?" Alfie grinned. Gerald was thrilled he loved this game, so simple but such incredible fun. The fields near his terraced home had the most fantastic hills, whose steepness cried out for being rolled down at endless speed. At the mere suggestion that they should play the game, they raced through the long grass and across the open fields to the top of the tallest hill. Breathless they shouted at the top of their voices, "Sound your holler!" as they rolled down one side of the hill and scrambled up the other. They played for hours racing down the hill by launching their bodies into an over and over rolling motion laughing joyously as they went.

"This is great," Clive sighed, as he lay flat on his back exhausted at the bottom of the hill. The fields and woods were a haven for a small child and the freedom was intoxicating, especially to the Challenders who had less independence at home. It wasn't that they didn't live near the countryside; it was that their father was extremely strict and gave them very little freedom.

"We're not allowed to do this at home," Josie said sadly.

"Why not? It's fun!" Gerald asked surprised.

"Because we're 'Challenders,'" she mimicked.

"And don't we know it," Clive chimed in as he clawed angrily at the grass. Their dad still acted like a police sergeant and expected them to behave impeccably; by all accounts they had to stick religiously to the rules. Gerald observed his middle cousin as he saw frustration flash across his face. He could see why Clive loved his summers so much and perhaps understood why he got up to so many tricks during his stay. Vic Challender was not a man who tolerated bad behaviour and would have scolded Clive dearly if he knew the truth about his capers during his vacation. Eileen feared her husband's wrath as well and was resolute when it came to keeping secrets from her husband.

The evening was fast approaching and Gerald looked anxiously down at his wristwatch, he desperately wanted to go to Albert's house and see how Douglas was doing. Gerald had shared most things in the past with his cousins, but he thought about Clive's cruel streak and Josie's tendency to blab to get attention, and wondered whether he'd ever be able to share his special friend with them. Tired and hungry, the cousins jovially made their way back to the small house on Richmond Street, no barriers existed between them, they were all united in the joyous day that they had had.

"Where you lot been?" Florence cursed at the top of her voice, as the group of children all trundled into the house. "Better take them dirty shoes off and get them hands washed before tea." The children did as they were bid and scurried into the kitchen to wash up before they ate.

After dinner when their bellies were full to the brim, the children disbanded from their group in search of different stimulation. Josie chose to snuggle in between her two eldest cousins. Revelling in all the attention little girls get from young women, she watched happily as they showed her how to sew and praised the creative child on her quick learning. Alfie and Clive's duo reformed quickly and they wasted no time in sneaking off out the back. Seeing that the boys were out of earshot, Gerald seized his opportunity to speak to his mother.

"Mam," he said quietly, as he approached her at the kitchen sink.

"Yes duck, what is it?" she said not flinching a muscle.

"I'm just off to Albert's, to check on that animal we found," he winced as the lie rolled convincingly off his tongue.

"Alright sweetheart but take Susan with you will you, everyone else is busy." Gerald tipped his head back in dismay and let out a small sigh. "Oh don't be mean Gerald, Susan likes animals," his mum said in response to his reaction.

"I do like animals," Susan grinned as she entered the kitchen.

"Come on then Suze, let's go," Gerald said as he grabbed his cousin's arm and dragged her outside.

While they walked, Susan was persistent in her inquisitions. "What kind of pet is it?" "Where did you find it?" "Has it got a name?" After several minutes of constant badgering, Gerald had had enough.

He stopped dead in his tracks and turned to Susan, "Listen Suze, before we get to Albert's there's summat I need to tell you."

Seeing her cousin's concerned expression, Susan turned to look at Gerald and smiled, "It's OK, you can tell me."

"This animal we found, isn't a... well... an animal, he's a... he's a..." Gerald stammered.

"He's a what?" Susan encouraged.

"He's an insect," Gerald blurted out as he strode ahead.

"An insect? What kind of insect?" Susan asked intrigued as she chased after him.

Gerald turned and looked at his cousin. He had been relieved that it was Susan who had joined him, rather than any of the others. He smiled as he admired her beautiful kind face now aglow with curiosity; instantly he knew he could trust her. Aunty Eileen always said she was like the secret service when it came to keeping secrets, no amount of bribery or torture would make her tell. Gerald recalled how she'd kept quiet about all of Clive's escapades in the past and he saw no reason to doubt that she would break his confidence either.

Satisfied that his secret would be safe, Gerald slowly began to unfold the story of how he'd found Douglas; he described his magical qualities and how he had started to communicate with him. Susan had been sceptical at first, as she too had fallen for his tricks in the past, but Gerald was so genuine that she had to believe him. He explained that he didn't know what to do next or why Douglas was here, but he did know that it was important.

"How long ago did you find Douglas?" Susan asked.

"This'll be the fourth day!" Gerald replied.

"Maybe not long then!" she said, sure that Gerald knew what she meant.

"What do you mean?" he retorted anxiously.

"Before he turns into a chrysalis, of course!" Susan stared at her cousin in disbelief. "Don't you know the lifespan of a caterpillar?" Gerald shook his head, still shaken from the proclamation. Susan put on her schoolmarm voice and cleared her throat. "We learnt it at school," she said, very pleased with herself that she was able to spout yet another fact that Gerald didn't know. "Ahem," she began as she cleared her throat again. "Caterpillars hatch from eggs then they eat and eat and eat until they get fat. Then, when they have shed their five layers of skin, they go to sleep in their chrysalis."

"What happens then?" Gerald asked with interest.

Happy that she was centre stage, Susan continued, "They nibble their way out of their cocoon and become a magnificent butterfly or moth depending on the type." Gerald was delighted at the thought that Douglas would make a magnificent transformation into a beautiful butterfly. Transfixed he listened to his informative cousin as she went into detail about the whole process, but his joy soon turned to horror when she concluded her science lesson and told him that the beauty didn't last for long as a butterfly's life was very short.

"How short?" Gerald said beginning to panic.

"It depends on the size, type and time of year that it was born really, but generally no longer than a month or so," she concluded. Gerald thought about Douglas and how big he was now and grinned, he'd surely live for the longest time, especially during such a glorious summer. "What's so funny?" Susan asked.

"Oh it's complicated," he said thoughtfully. He looked ahead towards Albert's house and in the distance he could see his friend standing in the doorway. "Come on we're nearly there and then you can see for your sen!"

Albert, who had seen the two cousins approaching, had come to greet them. As they got nearer he beckoned to them to hurry, the pair could see that he was excited and Susan quickened her pace, but Gerald sped ahead to reach him first. Following Albert, he rushed through the door and through to the back room. There sitting amongst Albert's books, no longer housed in a jam jar and no longer able to crawl along the twig that Albert had carefully picked for him, was Douglas. Gerald couldn't believe his eyes, he could see why it wasn't practical for him to be incarcerated in the jar any longer and he smirked at the tiny twig, which would no longer bear his weight.

"Fabulous isn't he, Gerald?" Albert chirped excitedly.

"He's amazing!" Gerald gasped.

"Who's amazing?" Susan said breathlessly as she burst exhaustedly into the room.

"Susan," Gerald said proudly, "Meet Douglas!" Susan, in a very matter-of-fact manner stepped in between the observers and stared down at the creature in front of her.

"Gosh... he's... huge!" she said understanding why Gerald had been amused. Douglas was not only different in stature, now being the size of a small mouse, his features were sharper too. His green eyes shone brightly like precious emeralds which were only obscured by the dark black rims which now protruded from his face. Gerald noticed, that they were no ordinary goggles; they were actual flight goggles only a miniature version. The tiny dots which had once been on 15 of the 16 feet were gone, leaving the black dancing shoes to shine brighter than ever. The shoeless foot, was healed now, but still bare and Gerald wondered where the shoe could be?

Susan was speechless, but Gerald was enthralled. He stepped closer to the curious creature who, on seeing his friend approach, smiled so brightly that the tips of the fine hairs which covered his body glowed radiantly with joy. Gerald reached out his young hand and without hesitation Douglas stepped aboard, as if his carriage had arrived. Gerald wasn't afraid, he was captivated, he gazed deeply into the emerald eyes of the small creature and he listened intently through the silence not once breaking their connection.

As the minutes passed, tears began to roll gently down Gerald's cheeks and his face became drawn and pale. He spoke no words but his face reflected a picture of sorrow. Concerned for her cousin's welfare, Susan stepped forward and took Douglas gently from Gerald's grasp and placed him back amongst the books. Gerald, once released from his trance, stepped backwards and collapsed into a heap on a nearby armchair.

Susan hadn't felt what Gerald had felt but she'd seen the effect that it had on her dear cousin and it gave her cause for concern.

"I really do think that it would be best if I keep Douglas here again overnight, do you not agree?" Albert whispered to Susan as they both glanced at Gerald.

"I think that's a good idea," she mused, puzzled by Gerald's reaction. "Gerald what happened?" she quizzed as she bent down to comfort him.

"I don't know," he replied weakly.

"What is he Albert?" she asked as she gestured towards Douglas.

"We have yet to find that out my dear, but he seems to have a real bond with young Gerald." Susan left her cousin's side and walked steadily towards the resting creature. Keen to see if the magic was just for Gerald, she gently stroked Douglas' fur but no radiant glow came beneath her fingertips and the caterpillar's dazzling eyes seemed very ordinary when she glanced into them.

Exhausted from his encounter, Gerald was left to sleep for over an hour, his dreams plagued with images that he didn't understand. He knew that the feelings coming from the small creature were meant for him and him alone, but he didn't understand why or what Douglas was trying to tell him. When he awoke, Gerald crept towards Douglas and gazed upon his friend's ever-changing frame. Now sound asleep, no doubt tired from the intensity of their encounter, Gerald watched Douglas as he breathed deeply in his slumber. He'd never felt properly loved before, but he felt loved now. His mum had always cherished him, but her heart had been so broken that he never felt the real intensity of her love.

"Ah you're awake," Susan grinned, relieved to see the colour returning to his cheeks.

"Yeh felt a bit weird there for a bit," he sighed.

"Well it's late; we'd better be off before your mum wonders where we are and sends out a search party," Susan said, as she lifted Gerald to his feet and ushered him out of the door.

"What about Douglas?" Gerald yelped, momentarily grasping the architraves of the door frame.

"He'll be staying with me for the evening," Albert nodded. "He won't come to any harm, here with me," he added kindly. Gerald knew that to be true and he trusted Albert. Content that his small kindred spirit was once again in safe hands they bid Albert farewell until tomorrow and exited the small room.

Outside in the warm summer evening, Susan reached for Gerald's hand and squeezed it tightly; he returned her grasp with a gentle squeeze of his own.

"Come on," she said. "Let's go home." They walked steadily back to Gerald's terraced house, made their excuses to Florence when they arrived and elected to go straight to bed, stating that they were tired after the journey. The two children finally parted ways at their bedroom doors but before they entered their separate rooms, Susan turned to Gerald and took both his hands in hers.

"Your secret is safe with me you know Gerald and if there's anything I can do to help, just ask OK?" Satisfied that he knew this to be true Susan disappeared behind the wooden door, leaving Gerald on the landing.

Feeling exhausted too, Gerald walked slowly into his bedroom and crawled fully clothed into bed. He closed his eyes and thought about his episode with Douglas, he wasn't sure what had happened but the memory had left him with an overwhelming feeling of sadness and remorse. Gerald reflected on the emotions that he had experienced that afternoon and as much as it tired him to feel like that, he felt prepared to accept that there was certainly more to come. Steadily Gerald drifted off into a deep slumber, his dreams free once again from his concerns.

Day Five
Mischief and Mayhem

Gerald woke with a heavy heart, as his encounter with Douglas came to the forefront of his mind. Recalling Susan's account of the life cycle of a caterpillar, he pondered what day five of Douglas' life would bring and wondered how many days he would have left before he became a chrysalis. Still wearing yesterday's clothes, Gerald rolled lifelessly out of bed and gazed sleepily around the empty room. Gerald shook his head in disbelief, wondering how it was possible for him to sleep so soundly when his siblings were so loud and boisterous. Rubbing his eyes with the back of his hand to bring them back to life, Gerald thought about how tired he had been recently.

"I don't normally sleep so much," he yawned to himself. Gerald had always been a lively child, never content to sit still. He didn't feel ill, but the episodes with Douglas were draining him more than he realised.

Hungry and weary from the day before, Gerald left his room and headed down the stairs in search of food. A magnificent aroma of freshly baked bread greeted his nostrils as he entered the parlour.

"Morning sleepyhead," Florence smiled kindly at her young son and gently kissed him on top of his head. "You alright Gerald? You're sleeping so much, you're going miss half your summer," she told him affectionately.

"Yeh I know. Where is everyone Mam?"

She filled a small mug with milk and handed Gerald a large round of bread and jam and said, "Up fields of course, they've been out since seven o'clock, eat up and you can go and meet up with them." Hungrily, Gerald tucked into the soft slice, which was thinly spread with sweet sticky jam and watched with interest as his mother danced and swayed around the kitchen as she sang sweetly to herself.

Gerald had only ever seen her sing once before, but he wondered what had made her so happy today. He wiped his mouth on the back of his hand, sloshed down the cool milk and stood to leave in search of his cousins. Before he had chance to go, his mother got hold of his arm to stop him, reached inside her apron pocket and pulled out a letter.

"Albert's left you a note," she said as she handed the small brown envelope to him.

"As he been here this morning then?" Gerald enquired, beginning to understand the reasoning behind her pleasant mood.

"Yeh, he stayed for a bit, while your Anty Eileen went to butcher's for me."

Satisfied that her motherly job was done, Florence patted her son on his shoulder and with her wicker washing basket on her hip, left the kitchen to continue with her other domestic chores.

"Did he say ought else?" Gerald yelped after his mother.

"Yeh, he said he were sorry but it couldn't be helped," Florence hollered in response. Gerald frantically opened the letter. Contained within it was Albert's explanation that he had to go to London for a few days, and a request to call on him later that day to make the arrangements for Douglas. He knew that his absence meant that the injured pet would need to be looked after elsewhere for a while until he returned, but Gerald hoped that Albert had thought of an alternative place for Douglas.

Fearful that Albert had not had the time to come up with a strategy for Douglas, Gerald began to fret, tightness grew in his chest and a sense of urgency and dread ran through him.

"Where am I going put him now?" he whimpered to himself. Gerald slumped back down on to the kitchen chair and laid his weary head on the table while he thought. Where could he be safe? Who could help him? Who would keep his secret? He'd already trusted Albert and Susan but now he needed yet another adult. He so wanted to confide in his mum, but home wasn't safe while Clive and Alfie were there. There was only one person who could help him and that was his Aunty Aggie. "Her house be safe," he said as he thought out loud. She only had Uncle Alan and Grandpa Hughes. There was Kim of course, but she'd be no bother. Gerald had to tell Susan the news, so he made haste to the fields to find her.

It didn't take long to hear the echoes of children's laughter resonating across the hills.

"Come on Gerald, where've you been?" his cousins called as they saw him approach. The children were lapping up yet another glorious summer's day, splashing about in the small stream which ran along the back of the fields. At that moment Gerald's concerns disappeared and he embraced the simplicity of his childhood.

"You could have woke me!" he joked as he raced towards them. Alfie and Clive were skimming stones; Josie and Susan were shoeless bathing in the cool stream. Gerald kicked off his shoes and socks and slid his toes into the chilly water next to Susan and Josie. "What are plans for today then?" he asked cheerily.

Excitedly, Josie launched her hand up really high, like she knew the answer in class. "Ooh I know. Why don't we go and play in the den that we found last summer?" she said enthusiastically. Susan turned, to her little sister horrified.

"OH NO! No, no, no," she said sternly. The boys began to snigger.

"Why not?" Josie said stamping her feet.

"Don't you remember last time we played there, you decided to decorate the walls with the cowpats," she said remembering the episode very vividly.

"Oh yes, sorry. I decorated you too didn't I? Sorry," Josie said as she batted her eyelashes apologetically.

"Well, I don't know about you lot, but Alfie and I are up for some real adventure this summer," Clive said boastfully as he nodded to Alfie. Gerald didn't know what his cousin's plans were, but he sensed that there would undoubtedly be mischief.

"What are you up to this time Clive?" Susan reprimanded. Clive dropped the remainder of his pebbles in the stream and turned to face his older sister.

"Today is the day I am going to outwit old man Johnson," he said proudly.

"What do you mean outwit Mr Johnson, you know what happened last year," Susan said scornfully.

"Yes we all know what that bully did to me last year and this year he'll pay for it," Clive seethed.

"I'll help you Clive," Josie piped up anxiously drying her feet on her underskirt.

"Excellent little sis, anyone else want to help?" Gerald looked nervously at Susan who was glaring at Clive. This was his chance to be part of the boys' brigade. He knew if he bailed now there'd never be another opportunity, and before he knew it, the words had flown out of his mouth and he'd volunteered.

"I'm in Clive."

"Well, well, well, little Gerald mixing with the bad boys. OK you're in, but it's a big secret, we all have to make a pact."

"Ahem, you're forgetting me Clive," Susan said, in her authoritative tone.

"Oh come on Suze, I have it all planned out I promise," Clive pleaded.

"What if it all goes wrong Clive? Mum won't be able to keep it from Dad this time!" she shrilled.

"Tell you what, you can be the foreman and if there's any sign of things not going to plan, I'll stop, OK?" Susan liked the idea of being in charge and once she'd agreed to be part of the pact, she was in. "OK that's great," Clive said excitedly. "It's going to work like a dream, now I have all you lot to help." The children huddled together to hear Clive's master plan.

"This heist is going to be the best in the history of scrumping and I don't want anyone to miss it," Clive beamed. "Susan, you need to go to Uncle Alan's shop and borrow a crate, big enough to give me the height needed to reach the tree over their fence. Alfie, fetch my scrumping machine." Gerald stood in line and waited for his job, he had no illusions that it would be the worst job. "Gerald I need you to fetch the coal sacks that Alfie and I stole and hid behind the shed on Grandpa's allotment."

"That's a really dirty job Clive," Susan said, annoyed that he'd purposely chosen Gerald to do it.

"I know it is sis, I'd do it myself but I have a few things to do first before we can start."

"Don't worry Gerald, I'll help you, I don't mind getting dirty," Josie interrupted.

"See, problem solved," Clive said, as he winked at his little sis. The children stood in a circle and linked arms as they made a family pact never to tell and they all promised that if anything went wrong, they'd just bolt. "OK, rendezvous in the lane behind the bus shelter around the corner from the Johnson's residence at 9.30 a.m." Clive ordered, as they disbanded the group. "And don't be late, timing is everything today," demanded Clive.

The Johnson's had a house just on the outskirts of town and although they had a big plot, they were not keen gardeners, much of it was unkempt, littered with weeds and rubbish. Nestled in amongst the clutter and overgrown garden, there was a small orchard which housed several fruit trees. The pear tree, which stood nearest to the house, was barren after a severe pruning from the old man, so no longer produced any fruit. The plum tree had contributed towards prizewinning pies in the past but the wasps, attracted by all the rubbish, had infested it for the third year running so that lay dormant as well. At the far end of the orchard nearest to the fence, stood the only thing in the garden that the Johnson's gave any attention to and you could tell; it was a beautiful sight. The large apple tree had a sturdy stance and a healthy array of branches which displayed luscious green leaves. From its many branches dangled ripe, ready to pick, succulent apples.

The old woman was immensely proud of her tree. The fruits of her labours gave her much joy every year as she won trophies after trophies at the village fete. This year, Mrs Johnson had her sights set on a bigger prize. Every decade the Women's Institute had a national baking competition which had the benefit of a large cash prize. Mrs Johnson had been thrilled when she was told the news that the winner of the village fete would be automatically entered. She had not been living in the village when the last one had taken place and she doubted very much in her ageing years that she would see another one. Mr Johnson, confident that his wife was sure to win again for the tenth time, was ecstatic, his wife would be in a constant jolly mood and he would have some peace for a while.

It was always Clive's intention to try and strip the tree of fruit, to prevent the famous apple pie from reaching the oven in time for the summer fete, but this news was an added bonus. Clive was intent on seeking his revenge and if he was going to make the old man pay, he'd have to smash the old lady's dream of national success, making it look like it was entirely her husband's fault in the process. Clive had watched the comings and goings of the Johnsons intently during his last two miserable days of last summer. The old woman went out on a Friday morning at 8.00 a.m. She had returned after lunch and had rowed with her husband, complaining of his drunkenness and laziness for sleeping all afternoon. Clive had seen this as the perfect time to hand over the booze that Eileen had promised Mr Johnson last summer.

Clive watched Mrs Johnson as she boarded the 8.15 a.m. bus into Nottingham city centre. Confident that she was gone until lunchtime, he steadily walked to the Johnson's front door. Clive knocked and Johnson thinking it was his wife, wasted no time in opening it.

Shocked to see the small stature of a young boy standing on his front porch and not his wife, Johnson bellowed, "What do you want?" Clive said nothing he simply wheeled the keg of beer in front of him that his mother had promised last year. Instantly remembering the gesture that Eileen had made, he grinned enthusiastically. "Oh right, that's lovely. All square then now lad, are we eh?" Johnson said, as he dragged the ale into his house. Eileen had told Clive that she expected him to be courteous when he handed over the ale.

Clive had been resistant to being so polite to such an abusive man, but he saw the advantage in Johnson truly believing that this was a truce and so in his most convincing voice he said, "Yes Mr Johnson, I am so sorry for my behaviour last summer, I can assure you that I have learnt my lesson and I won't be scrumping again." Johnson pursed his lips together and nodded, pleased that his dictatorial punishment had transformed Clive's character. Clive's courteous and apologetic manner gave Johnson no reason to suspect otherwise.

Clive bid Mr Johnson farewell and when he was sure that he was no longer looking, he hid out of sight in the bushes. Prudish by nature, Johnson's wife indoctrinated a lifestyle that was free from the vices that most men liked to partake in and wouldn't allow booze in her house. For a quiet life old man Johnson went along with his wife's demands, but he was a weak man and couldn't resist drink if it was put in front of him. Clive had seen Sydney hide bottles of beer in his garden and sneak out for crafty drinks when he didn't think his wife was watching, so he knew that the big man would consume the keg before his wife came home for fear that she'd make him discard it. Clive knew that it wouldn't take long before Johnson became intoxicated; he was a binge drinker and would have wanted to sleep off the effects, before his wife came home.

After an hour's waiting Clive was confident that Johnson would be in a drunken stupor and in a deep slumber but he had to be certain that he couldn't be woken. Cautiously Clive emerged from the bushes from outside the Johnson residence and approached the front porch. He banged loudly on the front door and then quickly ran back to the bushes and waited. To Clive's delight there was no answer. He did it again to be sure, but nothing stirred. Clive peered through the half-drawn curtains and saw Johnson flat out on the sofa with the keg toppled over on the floor. Unsure whether he was asleep, Clive pushed open the front door and listened, only the sounds of loud snoring seeping through the house could be heard.

Triumphant Clive quickly sped round to the bus shelter to collect his comrades. Susan and Alfie were already there as they had the least distance to travel, but Josie and Gerald had not yet arrived.

"What time is it?" Clive asked Susan anxiously.

Susan looked down at her wristwatch and sighed, "9.30!"

"I knew I couldn't trust Gerald! Bet he's blabbed!" Clive cursed.

"They had a long way to go you know!" said Susan, vexed in their defence.

"Come on, we'll have to get started without them," Clive urged, as he retrieved his invention from Alfie. As the trio approached the back of the house, Susan spotted Gerald and Josie bringing the sacks across the fields.

"Here they are Clive," she shouted brightly.

"Come on you're late," Clive shouted feeling relieved that Susan was right. Within seconds, the tardy duo greeted the others.

"Sorry Clive," Gerald said breathlessly, as he dropped the sacks on to the ground. "Grandpa were there, so we had to wait till he fell asleep before we could get sacks," said Gerald.

"He thought you'd blabbed!" Alfie teased.

Gerald looked hurt at Clive. "I wouldn't do that Clive, we made a pact!"

Clive shrugged his shoulders, "Come on let's get to work!"

Carefully, Clive assembled his invention, he grinned menacingly at it, as pure vengeance glistened in his eyes. The mechanism was constructed out of a piece of pipe which had a length of wire running through it from one end of the pipe to the other. At the controlling end attached to the wire there was a handle made from a piece of wood and at the far end, Clive had bent the wire to form a noose. Across the pipe at the noose end was a further piece of wire forming a T-bar which both prevented the noose from pulling right through when the wire was pulled and ensured that the fruit's stalk got severed, detaching it from its branch and ensuring its descent. The fruit was securely caught by an old fishing net, which had been firmly attached with tape to the underside of the pipe.

The clever gadget meant that with the simplest tug of the attached wire, Clive could pluck the fruit from the tree at a distance and gather his haul safely without detection. At quarter to ten, he was set. The crate that Susan had found and brought was propped up against the fence so that it didn't slip, the filthy coal sacks were stacked up on top of each other ready to be filled and the scrumping device was ready for action.

Clive was crazy with excitement as he mounted the crate and exclaimed, "Let the scrumping commence!"

Clive had scrutinised the tree, identified which apples could be reachable and determined how many he would need to take to ensure that the old lady would not be able to pull in her crop this year. As the competition was a national event and the stakes high, Mrs Johnson had baked extra pies in her zest for perfection and ultimate glory, so the apples were not as readily available as they had been in previous years. This had cheered Clive up no end, as it made his task much easier than he had first anticipated.

The arrogant cook had only left enough reachable apples on her tree for a few more pies and Clive was determined to get them all.

With all his siblings present, Clive studied the tree carefully. "There's no apples round the other side, she's used them all," he said, grateful that he didn't have to enter the garden. Carefully he lifted his invention over the fence. Slowly at first, he threaded the pole through the branches in search of his prize. He steadily hooked his first apple, pulled the wire which snapped the apple's stalk, dropping it blissfully into the net.

He hauled it back securely, passed it safely to Alfie, who cheered, "That's brilliant!" as he dropped it in the sack. After scrumping a few apples, Clive grew in speed and confidence. "To your right Clive," Alfie instructed as Clive scoured the tree for the best pick.

"I see them, there's a good cluster there," he shot back. One by one he meticulously readjusted the noose into a loop and continued to pluck, capture and bag all those apples which were visible and reachable into the sacks he'd pinched.

Susan was given the task of timekeeper, as the job had to be finished before the booze had worn off and the old lady had returned from the shops.

"You alright Clive? You've been at it for an hour, now," Susan said as she glanced down at her watch.

"I'm OK, just keep telling me where the reachable apples are," he said a little jaded.

"There's some right in the middle that she'd be able to grab, try and get those," Josie instructed, as she helped guide the pole to their position. As the heist went on for another half hour, Clive began to tire, his once steady hand was starting to waiver and beads of sweat were becoming visible on his forehead and underarms. The immense heat made it a difficult job, but Clive was determined. The odd apple started to fall to the ground.

"I think you should quit now Clive, it's nearly twenty past eleven," said Susan, "And if you drop any more apples the whole thing would have been pointless!"

"Yeh old woman could bake pie just by gathering them up off floor!" Alfie chimed in. Clive saw their point, but not wanting to risk any chance that Lorna Johnson could bake a pie, he leaped over the fence and collected the stray apples off the ground in his shirt.

"There," he said victoriously, as he clambered back over the fence and dropped them into the sack. "She's got no chance now!" he grinned.

Satisfied that he'd done enough, the children started to pack away.

"Where's the rope?" Clive asked as he looked at Gerald.

"I... I... Dint bring any, you dint say to," Gerald stuttered annoyed with himself that he'd forgotten.

"Oh don't fuss Clive," Josie said as she pulled hers and Susan's ribbons from their hair. "We'll use these."

Tightly strewn up with ribbon, the children tried lifting the sacks, but they were so full to the brim, that it made it impossible for them to be carried.

"How we going to move them, when we can't even lift them?" Clive said as he clasped his head in his hands.

"Praps we could roll them?" Alfie suggested.

"Shall we hide them here?" Susan said pointing to the bushes.

"No, too close for comfort, this has all been for nothing!" Clive ranted.

"Er Clive, we could er use..." Gerald tried to interrupt, but Clive just dismissed him completely. Amongst the panic and commotion the loud high-pitched voice of Josie rose above them all.

"I've got a good idea!" she said smugly as she glanced a knowing smile at Gerald. "Why don't we just use my trolley?"

"What trolley?" Clive said in a frustrated tone. Josie proudly and smugly picked up the string of her makeshift trolley and wheeled it out in all its glory for them all to see.

"That's what I was trying to tell you Clive," Gerald said disappointedly.

"The sacks were too big for me to lift, so Gerald made this for me from the stuff hanging around Grandpa's allotment, clever isn't he?" she said grinning at Gerald. Clive ran towards the contraption, sat on it and rocked it from side to side.

"Will it take the three sacks' weight?" he questioned Gerald.

"I should think so," Gerald enthused, chuffed that he was being championed.

"Come on then, what we waiting for?" Clive said as he applauded his young sister on her fantastic plan.

"Nice one Gerald," the cousins said, as they gratefully loaded the sacks of apples on to the trolley. Satisfied that their mission was complete, they made for home, confident that they had completed the heist without detection.

Gerald had enjoyed the time with his cousins, their carefree mischief and antics had given him a much-needed distraction and he felt really accepted by Clive for the first time. As he revelled in his newfound friendship, Douglas came to the forefront of his mind once again. The emotion he felt when he'd seen him last had left him feeling a little shaken and unsure of what was coming next.

Albert had said he was leaving on the Saturday afternoon for London to sign some documents. Gerald wondered what could be so important that he'd have to abandon both him and Douglas when he needed a friend so badly to help him. He broke loose from the group without much notice; they were all so busy congratulating Clive on his victory that it made it easy to slope off undetected. He quickened his pace knowing that the afternoon was fast approaching and he wanted to talk to Albert before he left for his train. After half an hour or so, Gerald reached Albert's house, knocked once and pushed open the front door.

"It's only me," he shouted to Albert, but the welcoming voice that replied was different, it wasn't a voice that he knew but it felt familiar all the same. Gerald made haste through the front room towards the rear, where Douglas had been, only to find him no longer there. In shock he took several wobbly steps backwards, only to be caught in the arms of Albert standing in the doorway.

"Steady there young man," Albert said, as he helped Gerald regain his balance.

"Is there someone else here?" Gerald asked, confused.

"No, just you and me, oh and Douglas of course!" replied Albert. Gerald looked at Albert in dismay. If it hadn't been him that had replied to his call, who had it, been? Or had he imagined it?

"Where's Douglas?" Gerald asked anxiously. Albert quickly put his mind at ease by gesturing towards the munching caterpillar. Douglas had overnight gained even more weight; it seemed his appetite was unquenchable, as he continued to crunch through more crisp green leaves.

Gerald stood back and admired the fine looking creature; his multi-coloured coat glowed radiantly like it had a point to make and his quizzical shoeless foot stood proud against the others. Gerald wondered where his missing shoe could be and if it would ever be found? Sensing Gerald's presence, like a baby does its mother, Douglas abandoned his feast and turned to smile magically at his special friend. Gerald had so many questions he wanted to ask his small companion, but without a voice, he feared he'd never hear the answers. He took the creature lovingly in his hands and gently stroked the glistening fur which ran across his back, while he thought. Douglas purred with delight at the gentle and soothing touch as Gerald's mind began to fill with memories from long ago.

The memories were full of joy and laughter, of love, devotion and of family. The dreamlike thoughts were of a happy time, before war came and lives were lost forever. His thoughts were filled with the love that surrounded a united couple and their young family. Gerald smiled at the unfamiliar but joyful scenes which filled his mind; he felt an overwhelming longing to stay in the trance-like state forever. The voice that he'd heard when he entered Albert's house, spoke again. The familiar sound was intoxicating as it whispered his name. Gerald began to feel giddy and his small frame weakened, breaking him free from his trance. Feebly, he placed his pet down where he had found him and sought comfort in the arms of Albert.

"What's wrong Gerald?" Albert asked.

"I don't know what he's trying to tell me," Gerald sniffed.

"One day you will Gerald, I'm sure of it," soothed Albert.

Exhausted from his trance and aware that Albert had a train to catch, Gerald made haste to stow Douglas away.

"I've put plenty of fresh green leaves in with him," Albert said as he handed Gerald Douglas' new carriage.

Fashioned especially for Douglas, Albert had hand carved a wooden box on which he'd expertly routed Douglas' name on the side and hand drilled several small holes in the lid so he could breathe.

"Thanks Albert," Gerald beamed.

"I know that it is not half as good as your dad could have done, but it will do," Albert said sadly.

"I think it's perfect," Gerald replied kindly, as he remembered his dad's expert craftsmanship.

"I'm sorry, I have to leave at such short notice Gerald, but it's urgent and I'm afraid it simply can't wait," Albert said, as he helped Gerald put Douglas in his knapsack. He didn't explain why he had to go to London so urgently, but Gerald could tell from his expression that it was necessary. "Have you considered where you will take him?" Albert asked.

"Thought me Anty Aggie might help me!" Gerald said hopefully.

"Ah yes Agatha, she'd have been my choice too!" smiled Albert, as he turned to see Gerald out of the door.

"I'll see you in few days then. Will you be back for match?" Gerald asked.

"Just remind me when that particular event is again?" Albert quizzed.

"Sunday of course!" Gerald shouted as he made his way towards his auntie's house.

"I will definitely try my very best to be in attendance!" Albert called after him. Gerald had seen no reason to seek further explanation when he had wished him a safe journey and a speedy return. He had wondered whether it was to do with his benefactor but decided that it was no business of his so had refrained from asking.

Gerald trundled across the fields towards his auntie's house, confident that his aunty would greet him with open arms when he stepped through the front door. The journey was tiresome, as he felt exhausted after his emotional interlude with Douglas and he was glad when he reached the stone steps of number 31.

"Oh, what a lovely surprise!" she said enthusiastically as her favourite nephew crossed the threshold. Gerald slipped off his knapsack quickly and placed it out of reach as Kim bounded towards him. Kim was Aunty Aggie's crazy Alsatian dog. When the door had opened, she had instantly awakened from her usual place in front of the roaring open fire and raced to the door to greet him. She, like his aunty, was very fond of Gerald and always greeted him with such gusto. "Leave poor lad alone Kimmy and get on your box," Aunty Aggie screeched. Kim obediently returned to her place of slumber, her tail still frantically wagging, her eyes fixed on Gerald. "You're filthy lad," she said. "Looks like you've been with coalman, whatever you been up to?" Aggie ruffled his blonde hair and hugged him affectionately. Ordinarily Gerald would have made up fabulous exciting tales, but today had been so wonderful he didn't need to. Clive had sworn him to secrecy though, in exchange for his inclusion in the heist, so Gerald couldn't divulge anything, but he did have his own secret to share.

His grandpa was having his afternoon nap on the couch and Gerald noticed that his uncle was yet again absent from the family home.

"Where's Uncle Alan?" he asked politely.

"Oh he's working lad, as usual. It's only two o'clock mind, he be back later." Uncle Alan was a workaholic, although he loved his wife dearly, he was not a naturally affectionate man and didn't pay his wife the attention that she craved. Aggie had suffered with ill health for most of her adult life and Alan had been her rock. She was a kind lady who, despite her problems, was still sympathetic towards other people and didn't dwell on the past. Gerald loved his aunty, she was fun and she always had time for her favourite nephew. He desperately needed her help now that Albert was gone and Douglas was homeless. She always said, "There's a solution to every problem you just need to find it". Gerald looked longingly at his aunty and hoped that she was going to do just that.

"You look bit tired lad," she said concerned for her nephew.

"I am a little," he said.

"You hungry?" she asked.

Gerald nodded, "Dint have any dinner."

"Too busy playing in them fields I bet," she replied knowingly. "Shall I draw you a bath first?" she said as she turned his hands over to examine their state. Gerald looked down at his soot-stained hands and shrugged his shoulders. "You'll have to help me fetch and carry water mind, my lungs not too good today," she coughed. Gerald collected his knapsack and left it at the bottom of the stairs out of sight of Kim and then followed his aunty into the kitchen and out into the backyard. "Can you get me that down," she said, as she pointed to the tin bath hanging on the wall.

"Yeh, I've done it loads of times for me Mam," he said, as he carefully detached the bath from its hook.

"Ready?" she said, as she bent her knees and straightened her back in preparation for lifting the cumbersome vessel.

The duo manoeuvred the bath into the kitchen and laid it to rest in front of the fireplace. Aunty Aggie groaned as she let go of the tin bath.

"You OK Anty Aggie?" Gerald asked concerned that she had overexerted herself.

"I'm alright sweetheart dunt you worry, I'll be right in a minute," she said, as she steadily inhaled and exhaled deep breaths. Slowly she made her way towards the sink and reached underneath. "Here, you need to fill them up from copper," she said holding out two sturdy buckets for Gerald to take. "You'll need four or five buckets, for a decent bath. I'll get fire going while you do that," she said. Gerald was thrilled he'd never been allowed to fill the bath before.

Gerald watched his aunty as she knelt in front of the fireplace and set to work building a fire. First she cleaned out the old ash from the grate and then expertly set the fire; within moments it was lit and roaring in the hearth. She dragged the metal fireguard in front of the fireplace and tidily cleared away all the ash with her dustpan and brush.

"Right," she said as she dusted her apron off. "Take them dirty clothes off and give them me, I'll rinse them through, then they'll be dry for morning and your Mam not know difference!" she winked knowingly at him. "Go on, in you get," she said smiling at his excitement.

Gerald did as he was bid and stepped into the scorching water; he revelled in the solitary bath with the fresh clear liquid rubbing up against his body. When he was fully submerged, she handed him a wooden scrubbing brush and a bar of Palmolive soap.

"You'll need them, state you're in," she laughed. He scrubbed himself clean and lathered the soapy bar all over his body. Tired after his eventful day, he lay back against the high end of the bath and sighed. As the youngest, he'd always had to be last in the communal bath at home; it was always dirty and slimy by the time he had his turn, so this was pure heaven. Kim brushed under his dangling fingertips and came to rest by the heat of the fire; dozily he drifted into a deep sleep.

"Come on ducky, let's get you out of water now before you catch your death," Aggie urged. Gerald must have been there for a while, the bath water was cold and his fingers had gone like prunes. "Let's get you wrapped up warm and fill your belly eh!" Gerald's Aunty Aggie said, as she motherly sheathed him in a fresh towel. Gerald took his place at the table and eagerly awaited his meal. Aggie filled a bowl with piping hot stew straight from the stove, accompanied by a chunky round of her home-cooked loaf. Gerald dipped his bread keenly into the stew and devoured it hungrily. "Good?" Aggie asked as she tucked into her own.

"Yeh, lovely ta," he beamed at her. The bread wasn't as good as his mum's, but he welcomed it all the same.

"I think its best if you stay for night Gerald, as it's getting late. I'll send word to your Mam when your Uncle gets home." Gerald felt tired again after his big meal and was grateful that he didn't have to go home and explain where he'd been all afternoon. He'd tackle his cousins early in the morning. Gerald looked at his lovely aunty and thought what a wonderful mother she would have made and wondered why she had never had children of her own. He thought of Douglas cooped up in his knapsack and wondered whether his secret could last another day. Believing that he needed to sleep on his words before he spoke to his aunty about Douglas, he rose from the table and gathered up his grandpa's spare nightshirt from the back of the chair.

"Thanks Anty Aggie," he said wearily, as he kissed her warm cheek. He walked over to the bottom of the stairs, collected his knapsack and climbed to the first floor to share a resting place with his familiar old room-mate, hopeful that his aunt would be as understanding in the morning.

Day Six

A Place to Hide

The morning had come quickly, Gerald had been so tired when he went to sleep that he'd not planned his speech. Eager to sort out the problem in his knapsack he crept out of the shared room still dressed in his grandpa's spare nightshirt and down the stairs into the kitchen where he found his aunty already busy with her chores. The kitchen was full of wet washing which she was systematically and proficiently pushing through the mangle. Gerald shuddered as he watched his aunty skilfully turn its handle to squeeze out the water and gravely rubbed his fingers in recollection of his own encounters with his mum's contraption.

Without saying a word Gerald withdrew the handcrafted wooden box out of the knapsack, placed it in the middle of the kitchen table and waited. Aggie, on seeing her nephew enter the room, stopped her work, picked up the small pile of neatly folded and freshly laundered clothes and with a kind smile handed them to Gerald.

"What's in box?" she asked very intrigued. Gerald simply reached over, slid back the lid of the box and revealed Douglas in all his glory.

His aunty was used to Gerald telling tales so was waiting for the next fanciful story to unfold but nothing could prepare her for something like this.

"He's real," Gerald said, as she stared disbelieving at the animated caterpillar. His Aunty Aggie clasped her hand over her mouth and began to chuckle nervously.

"He's incredible, where'd you find him?" Gerald was pleased with his auntie's reaction and was proud that he'd made yet another fine choice in trustworthy adults.

"I fount him six days ago near stream," Gerald confessed.

"He's very big for a caterpillar," his aunty said.

"He's got bigger every day!" Gerald said as he crouched down to peer at him too.

"Does your Mam know?" Aggie asked. Gerald closed his eyes and gently shook his head. "Well that's understandable, I suppose," she said giving his waist a gentle squeeze.

"Albert knows though! He's named him Douglas, after Douglas Bader."

"Yeh I can see resemblance to pilot me sen," she laughed. "Where's his shoe?" she said noticing his sixteenth bare foot.

"He's never had one, he were injured when I fount him."

Aggie stood up and stretched her aching back. "What do you need me to do?" she asked kindly. Gerald took a deep breath and looked his aunty in the eye and explained how he had kept him hidden at Albert's house, but now that Albert had had to go to London for a few days he needed somewhere else to hide him. He didn't mention the magical side of him; he'd do that later when he'd got his head around it himself.

"Well I'm touched that you thought of me to help you," she beamed. "I'm sure we can find somewhere to keep him safe lad." Gerald knew Aggie had hiding places for her secret vices, so was confident that Douglas would be well hidden. Aggie lifted her index finger to her cherry coloured lips and gently stroked her top lip in thought. "I could put him in me chocolate stash!" she said but then decided that he would be too cold right at the top of the pantry. "Too big now for matchbox in lavatory," Aggie laughed to herself. Gerald's shoulders rose guiltily. "Oh I see! Used that when he were small did we? Clever boy! I can see I'll have to move me smokes now then!"

One by one the secret hideouts were quickly dismissed, until Aggie thought of the perfect place.

"Oh yes... let's put him in there," she said wistfully, her blue eyes, just like his mother's, glazed over with tears, her youthful face groaned with anguish and pain.

"You OK Anty Aggie?" Gerald asked out of concern.

"Yes ducky, I'm all right. Come on follow me," she said as she lifted Douglas off the kitchen table in a dreamlike state and carried him up the stairs into her bedroom. She was unrecognisable; he'd never seen his aunty cry she was always so happy, so full of fun.

Aggie passed Douglas to Gerald, steadily bent down on all fours and pushed the metal-framed bed to one side. Under the bed, she worked free a loose floorboard revealing a spectacular hiding place which was full to the brim.

"I only come here in me darkest moments," she told Gerald. "Which thankfully aren't so many nowadays."

From inside the crevice Aggie pulled out the reasoning behind her tears. The space held the memories of a child lost. This sanctuary was where she went to remember and let out all her grief, Gerald thought, he felt saddened that his aunty had secrets that she couldn't share. He regarded his aunty as she thoughtfully removed the tiny unworn baby clothes and held them in her hands. She gently stroked the soft wool with her fingertips and wiped away the tears as they appeared in her eyes.

Carefully she lifted out the sympathy cards tied up in a ribbon and glanced at the kind words, a small sorrowful smile curled her upper lip and she reflectively placed them to one side. She studied the tiny ageing hospital name tag and turned to look at Gerald.

"They didn't even put baby's name on it, just Baby Jenkins! Don't suppose it matters now eh!" she sniffed as the tag joined the mounting pile next to her. "Oh dear this is worst bit," she said exhaling deeply. "Wrapped little mite in this, just before it had its last breath," she said as she withdrew a white crocheted blanket from its casket. She slowly lifted the woollen cloth up to her face and inhaled the sweet scent of her tiny child. "Still smells lovely, even after all them years," she said as Gerald swarmed in to comfort her. She patted Gerald's knee gratefully and placed the blanket to one side. She retrieved Douglas from Gerald's grasp, drew back her tears and said. "Let's see if he'll fit, shall we?" He did, perfectly.

She didn't explain anymore about the baby she'd lost, she must have thought Gerald was too young to truly understand. She simply hugged him tightly. Aggie gathered up her memories and stored them under her bed clothes in her chest of drawers. Wiping her eyes with her pinafore she tried to contain her heartache but Gerald could see the torture she felt. Gerald bent down to Douglas and stroked his small friend and thought about his auntie's inner battle. She was so lovely, he thought, he wished so much that she could have peace and hoped that one day she would.

"Come on duck," Aggie said regaining her composure. "Best leave him for now, check on him later eh?" Gerald helped his aunty pull back the bed frame, leaving the loose plank just resting above the hiding place. "Your secret's safe with me sweetheart," she assured him. Gerald had no doubt that it would be.

Happy that Douglas was in a safe haven and anxious that his cousins would be wondering where he'd been after the heist, he pulled on his freshly laundered clothes and ventured quickly out of the house. As he turned the corner out of his auntie's street and into his own he was surprised to be greeted by his cousins so early on the Saturday morning.

"Where've you been then?" Clive asked suspiciously. Gerald had to think quickly, the last thing he wanted was Clive discovering what he'd hidden at his Aunty Aggie's.

"Couldn't go home like I were, could I? I were filthy! Covered in soot from them coal sacks and I knew me Mam would have asked me a load of questions. So I went to see me Anty Aggie and she cleaned me up, now I'm good as new," Gerald said as he opened his arms to show off his clean clothes.

Clive looked suspicious and hissed through his gritted teeth, "You didn't tell her OUR secret did you?"

"Of course I dint tell her OUR secret!" Gerald replied honestly, he'd only shared his.

Half satisfied that Gerald was telling the truth Clive bent towards him and whispered, "We need you to help us move and hide the apples again, come on we need to be quick before anyone sees us."

Susan locked arms with Gerald and explained that after the heist, the children had gaily trundled across the farmland adjacent to the Johnson's field, and they'd got halfway across when they had been reprimanded by Mrs Osbourne, who lived at the farm.

"She'd craned her neck to see what we were pulling," crowed Josie.

"But we all crowded round the trolley so she couldn't get a peek," chimed in Susan, pleased that she had outwitted the nosey woman.

Sure that Mrs Osbourne, who was Mrs Johnson's old friend, would try to find out what they were doing, they'd had to think fast. They had decided to temporarily stash the apples while they thought of a permanent place to hide them.

"I told them to hide them in the cemetery!" Jodie chirruped.

"Is that where we're headed?" asked Gerald a little spooked.

"Yes. Don't worry, I won't let Clive trap you in a grave again, that was horrid," she said as she glared at her younger brother.

The cousins arrived back at the cemetery; they'd played in there so often that no one would be suspicious of them being in there for the second time in two days. Gerald followed his friends through the graveyard to 'the clump' at the very top. It was used for cemetery waste, dead flowers and general rubbish. Apart from the old gardener, who had a fire there weekly, and the occasional conscientious visitor, the site was usually empty. It had always been the perfect place for the children to hide in and not somewhere anyone would think to seek.

Keen to get going and continue with his brilliant plan, Clive beckoned his comrades to get to work. One by one they retrieved the three heavy sacks and one small bag from behind the big bushes, where they'd stashed them the day before, and heaved them on to the trolley, which was hidden separately.

"So what are we going to do with them now Clive?" Susan asked, not pleased that her usually immaculate attire was now soiled from the dirty sacks.

Clive laughed raucously, "We're going to bury them, right under the old bag's nose!"

He had conjured up the plan yesterday, when he had noticed a few empty graves opposite the Johnson's residence. The graveyard wasn't a huge facility, it only housed the deceased from the local area, it wasn't creepy or strange it was a peaceful place. The cousins had played in there so many times over the years, they'd hid behind the gravestones, ridden their bikes up and down the smooth wide paths. It was a playground to them and apart from Clive's prank on Gerald last year which had caused alarm, they did not see it as a scary place and the thought of burying the apples inside a grave didn't faze them, they all agreed it was a brilliant plan.

"Here this one will do," Clive motioned excitedly. The gang enthusiastically dragged the heavy load towards the nearest empty grave. "Come on Gerald, help me and Alfie shift the planks," Clive said. Gerald did not move, he was staring into the pit of the grave, all the anxieties of being trapped in there last summer returning to his subconscious. Clive walked across the planks, which lay across the gaping hole and came to rest by Gerald.

"I promise I won't push you in, OK!" he said, sure that if he didn't say something Gerald wouldn't be any help at all. Susan, worried that Clive wouldn't stick to his promise, pushed her brother out of the way.

"Leave him alone Clive, it's your fault he's frightened in the first place," she scowled. "He's bound to be frightened Clive!" Susan screeched as Clive shrugged his shoulders at her. "You sat on the planks and wouldn't let him out, for hours," she continued.

"Alright I know, I know. No need to go on about it Suze. Are you going help or not Gerald?" Clive yelped.

"Yes I'll help just don't want to go down ladder!" Gerald winced.

"I'll go down the ladder Clive," Josie volunteered enthusiastically.

"It's OK Jose," Clive smiled impressed with his kid sister's tenacity. "Better if I go down! I can make sure that we get an even spread of apples as they drop into the pit then."

Clive and Alfie moved the planks of wood to create a large enough gap for Clive to climb down through and he descended the wooden ladder and into the 12 ft double grave. Gerald and Alfie, who were less confident standing now on the edge of the deep grave, watched in awe as Clive made his eerie decent into the muddy ditch.

"It's perfect," he yelled from the depths of the trench. "Start pouring in the apples," he said excitedly as he waited eagerly at the bottom. One by one the three sack loads were poured quickly into the hole and then Clive strategically spread them across the bottom of the grave. Happy that the apples were evenly layered he calmly climbed out of the tomb and started to kick the mud that was piled up at the side of the grave into the crevice. "Come on then," he urged his cousins, "they need to be covered over or the plan will be flawed."

"OK genius," Susan jeered, put out that she hadn't thought of that.

Satisfied that they had done a fine job, the two elder boys slid back the planks, Josie stacked the empty sacks on to her trolley and Susan lifted its string ready to pull.

"What's that?" Clive shouted pointing at a small knapsack lying on the ground next to the grave. "Don't tell me we've missed some apples!" Clive said holding his head in his hands.

"No, not missed them, Clive," said Josie in an authoritative manner. "I saved them for the pie."

"What PIE?" said Clive starting to feel exasperated with his little sister.

"The pie mummy is going to bake with me for the village fete of course!" Relieved, Clive smiled a broad grin, strolled towards his kid sister and proudly kissed her cheek. "What's that for Clive?" Josie asked.

Taking her small hand proudly in his and shaking his head admiringly, "Brilliant!" he said, "Just brilliant, Josie."

The children were not the only ones to have risen early on the Saturday morning. Mrs Johnson had set to work in preparation for her challenge ahead. She'd baked so many pies she no longer needed a recipe it was all imprinted on her brain. The old lady was very superstitious. When she'd won her first prize at the fete, after several years of being runner-up at other fetes, she was convinced that she must have done something different. From then on every time she baked her competition pie, she did so in the exact same order, on the exact same day at the exact same time.

She rose early because it was the best time for baking and as her husband didn't usually wake up much before eleven o'clock, she knew that she wouldn't get disturbed. Dressed as usual in her pale blue, delicately flowered dress, which she had worn every year since the first winning bake, she made her way downstairs but by the time that she'd got to the bottom, she was out of breath. Although Lorna still had an enviable petite figure for her age and could still fit into the tiny dress, the old woman's love of tasting her own cakes had made her gain over a stone since she had first started baking ten years before. As such the dress was now over a size too small and pulled very tightly over her bosom, making it very difficult for her to breathe. Lorna had been annoyed when the buttoned front dress had bulged open, but she had persevered and squeezed herself into it anyway, for she secretly believed in magic and was a firm believer that the dress held magical qualities. Not wanting to diminish the magic in any way the pious woman never washed the dress, so it was covered in old mixture and smelt of rancid cake.

Despite her uncomfortable attire, when she got down the stairs into her parlour, she launched into her baking routine. She stoked her Rayburn oven so it was piping hot and set the kettle on it to boil. After selecting her utensils from the kitchen drawer, she laid them out in their exact places on the kitchen table, donned her baking apron and methodically weighed out all her ingredients. When she was all set, she took a mug, which was carefully stowed with a small bowl and spoon and carefully unwrapped them, taking care not to rip the tissue paper.

On hearing the kettle whistle, she took it off the stove and made herself a cup of tea. Methodically she weighed out one and a half ounces of porridge and poured it into a saucepan. From the kettle she added hot water and stirred systematically over the stove until it was nice and thick and piping hot. She spooned the porridge into the small bowl and used the same spoon to drop a dollop of sugar on the top. Mrs Johnson ate the oat feast messily and noisily, leaving remnants of the porridge hanging from her whiskers, which protruded from her upper lip and chin. After she'd had her fill, she carefully washed and dried the two crockery pots and spoon, wrapping them up neatly in the same tissue paper, and stowing them away safely in the same place ready for the next year.

Mrs Johnson was not a particularly fastidious person by nature, she was a lazy, selfish woman who was happy to let her husband fuss over her and do all the domestic chores. Gradually over the years, old man Johnson had become her slave in many respects and she had belittled him so much that he was now a shadow of his former self. However, when it came to baking her famous pie she was meticulous in everything she did and her minion was not allowed anywhere near her. Winning that competition meant everything. Before Mrs Johnson fetched and peeled her cooking apples from the magnificent tree she sat silently for a while and prayed. She had been always been a very religious woman and praying was an important part of her annual baking routine.

Mrs Johnson got up off her knees, dusted down her filthy dress, inhaled a deep determined breath and lifted her wooden bucket and placed it under her arm. She opened the back door and stepped outside into her garden in search of the juicy cookers. It was always Mr Johnson's job to collect the apples when she was doing her practice pies. Although Lorna did suffer from arthritis, she was an awful attention-seeker and a terrible hypochondriac. Her condition always seemed to worsen if she didn't like the look of a job or if Mr Johnson was on hand to do it for her.

Ordinarily she didn't pick the apples, as she claimed she couldn't manage to climb the steps with her arthritis, but miraculously she was always fit enough to do the same job on competition baking day. She made her way by memory across the unkempt orchard to where the prizewinning Bramley apple tree stood; she was terribly short-sighted and had forgotten to replace her glasses after praying. She placed her bucket on the ground; the wooden ladder was already resting against the broad trunk of her tree, no doubt put there by a doting Mr Johnson. She shook it gently to ensure its safety, lifted the hem of her dress, tucked it ungainly into her knickers and made her assent.

Mrs Johnson reached her bony fingers up to grasp an apple from its branch but all that she could feel were leaves. She peered closely at her precious tree and frantically pushed back the branches in search of her apples.

"Sydney! Sydney! Sydney!" she yelled at the very top of her voice, but no retort came. Mr Johnson was in a deep slumber. Annoyed that her calls had not been answered the old woman clambered quite nimbly down from the tree and sped rather swiftly across the garden and into the house for a woman with such ill health. "Sydney!" she bellowed. "Sydney wake up, wake up!" she demanded as she marched into the kitchen.

Grabbing her glasses off the table and firmly positioning them back on her face, she made haste up the stairs into their bedroom. Sydney was laying spread-eagled on their double bed with his face planted deep amongst the pillows.

"Wake up, you lazy brute, I need to talk to you!" Lorna screeched as she shook her husband awake.

Believing he was dreaming, old man Johnson growled at his wife, "Grwwwww go away!" But he soon came to when in her fury Mrs Johnson emptied the lukewarm contents of the chamber pot still stowed under the bed over his head.

"Aaaawwww what you do that for Lorna?" Sydney said in alarm.

"You weren't listening to me and I need to talk to you," she seethed angrily.

"What's wrong me love?" he swooned seeing that his wife was extremely irate.

"This!" she said pointing out of their bedroom window. The old man looked confused. Obediently he dragged his sodden body out of his bed and made his way to the window. Unlike his wife, Mr Johnson had very good vision and he could see immediately why his wife was so upset.

Apart from the odd apple bashed and bruised which lay uselessly on the ground, there hung from the splendid tree only one solitary remaining apple.

"Where have they all gone Sydney?" she bellowed. "They were all there on Friday morning when I went to the shops!" she screeched. Mr Johnson winced at her aggressive tone, he knew he'd get the brunt of this, he always did.

"I dunt know me darling. I really don't honestly know where they've all gone," he pleaded.

"Well you'd better get on and find them then, hadn't you!" Mrs Johnson shouted.

Dutifully Mr Johnson wasted no time at all in fetching PC Joyce from the station to investigate the matter. PC Joyce looked up at the empty apple tree and breathed a deep sigh.

"The most likely explanation I'm afraid to say it that they've been scrumped."

Lorna Johnson turned and glared at her husband. "This is all your fault!" Lorna seethed. "You were drunk again on Friday, weren't you Sydney?" she said as she raised her tiny fist at him.

"I'll speak to all the local parents in the area straight away Lorna," PC Joyce said, attempting to defuse the situation. "It can't be easy to hide all those apples!" he said as he disbelievingly surveyed the tree. Satisfied that someone other than her husband was on the case Mrs Johnson went back inside ranting crossly as she went.

As for Mr Johnson, he could do nothing but wait as PC Joyce had told him that there was little else that he could do. He understood that the police would have to be systematic in their search or run the risk of missing something but he felt useless, he had no idea where to look. Not wanting to go back into the house Sydney ventured over the field to his neighbours. Mrs Osbourne was away at her mother's for a few days but Farmer Osbourne would be there, he'd see if he had seen anything that could shed any light on the apples' disappearance on Friday.

From the clump at the top of the cemetery the children had heard Mrs Johnson's horrified screams and had hid immediately in the bushes to watch the whole scenario unfold. Clive grinned from ear to ear as he observed Mr Johnson get a browbeating from his wife. He sniggered as he casually walked away from the burning coal sacks and passed the apple-infested grave, satisfied that his task was complete. He didn't care that they would hunt high and low in search of both the culprit and the missing apples; he was convinced that they'd never find them.

Clive had smirked when he'd seen PC Joyce arrive on the scene, he knew he had history with his mum and she was his best advocate.

"Aren't you worried Clive?" Susan said as she reached his side.

"Nah, they won't find them Suze!" he said confidently. Smiling gleefully to himself Clive thought how it could take them days maybe even weeks to investigate the crime and he was certain that they'd never think to look in the grave, why would they? Mrs Johnson would be so miserable that she'd missed out on the fete trophy and the chance to win a cash prize at the national event, that she'd make her husband's life hell and Clive was beginning to feel satisfied that their war was almost over.

The cousins had been home a while when PC Joyce had arrived at their door.

"Hello kids are your mum's home? Just want to ask them a couple of questions!" PC Joyce was familiar with Clive and his summer antics so had made their house his first port of call. He'd had to speak to Eileen numerous times over the years about her wayward son, but Eileen had used the obvious affection he still held for his first love to her advantage and PC Joyce had always let it go. The girls had remembered to clean their face and hands but Clive's shoes were still covered in mud.

"Morning ladies," PC Joyce said in his official tone, determined not to let his harboured feelings for Eileen get in the way of his investigation this time. "There's been an incident of theft up at the Johnson residence which looks like a children's prank." Eileen immediately glared at Clive, who turned his head away so she couldn't see him.

"What's happened Tom?" Eileen smiled brightly, knowing full well that if it was Clive she'd have to use all her charms on her old flame.

"Mrs Johnson's cooking apple tree has been stripped bare!"

The sisters tried hard to disguise their amusement and even the policeman's lips curled up at the edge in acknowledgement of the irony. Eileen, who had designated herself as the spokeswoman, declared that they had neither seen nor had any apples in the house. PC Joyce, once again swayed by his affection for Eileen thanked them for their cooperation, smiled brightly at his old flame and looked knowingly down at Clive's filthy shoes. Eileen had reprimanded her children and Florence had scorned hers but the more they sought the truth the deeper the children hid their secret.

They had only a few days to wait and the apples would be gone forever, buried under the excessive weight of the local butcher who had died a few days before, it was a secret they'd have to keep forever.

"What about Josie's apples?" Susan had pointed out. "How are we going to explain those?"

The children looked towards the little girl who simply said in a most convincing voice, "You mean the apples I told Mum we'd got from Uncle Alan's grocery store?" The cousins once again stood back in admiration for the genius that was Josie.

Day Seven

The First Sunday

"Come on lads, up you get, service starts in half hour," Florence called from downstairs. Gerald, who was already awake, stared dismally out of the window. He disliked going to church. Half-heartedly he crawled out of bed and sauntered across the room to his sleeping siblings. Not wanting to upset Clive, Gerald chose to wake Alfie instead and leave Clive's disturbance to him.

"Mum's calling Alfie," Gerald said gently as he patted his brother's bare shoulder. "We've got to go to church," Gerald said glumly.

"What?" Alfie said as he yawned and stretched.

"Church Alf, it's Sunday," Gerald urged.

"Ohhhh, I hate church," Alfie groaned. Seeing that Clive was still fast asleep, Alfie casually launched his pillow across the room at him. "Get up Clive. We've got to go to Mass!" Clive rolled out of bed and lay face first on the bedroom floor.

"Morning has broken...!" Clive giggled as he warbled the song at the top of his voice.

Chivvied along by their terrible singing the boys dressed in their Sunday best.

"Ooh these flipping shoes," Gerald groaned as he tried to squeeze his ever growing feet into his tight shoes.

"Just slip them off during service and hook your feet under pew," Alfie said cringingly as he watched his kid brother cram his feet into the tight shoes.

"Not me Mam notice?" Gerald replied.

"Well she never noticed me do it," laughed Alfie as he walked out of the room. Gerald pulled off his shoes, tucked them under his arm and followed Clive and Alfie down the stairs.

"About time too," Eileen fussed as she brushed invisible bits of fluff off Clive's clothes. "We need to hurry if we're going to make Confession too," Eileen exclaimed.

"Confession?" Gerald gulped.

"Yes lad you won't be able to have your Communion without it," his Aunty Eileen said while she wiped the sleepy dust from Clive's eyes.

As much as Gerald disliked going to church, he did enjoy the hymns that they sang and the big family Sunday dinner that they had afterwards; but Confession was something that he detested. All the Hughes children went to the local Catholic school and Confession was a weekly occurrence. Always last in the queue with his palms sweating madly, Gerald would carefully plan out what he was prepared to divulge to the priest. He understood that the priest was god's servant but he couldn't get past the fact that he was just an ordinary man in a dog collar. Fearful that the priest would divulge all his secrets, he gave himself more penance than was dished out by the Lord, to make up for the untruths he told inside the confessional box.

Gerald had received his first Holy Communion in June of this year, so school holidays had never posed a problem before. His mother had agreed that as he had a weekly ritual at school this was a sufficient Confession to make. Gerald had been scared enough having Confession in a corner of the school hall but, he felt terrified at the prospect of having to do Confession in the big church.

"Oh do we have to go to Confession?" Clive moaned.

"Yes Clive you absolutely do!" Eileen replied sternly.

Eileen was a devout Catholic and insisted that her children always did Confession as she felt it cleansed their sole and she was determined to give Clive's regular cleansing. Gerald glanced at Alfie and Clive laughing jovially with the other cousins, clearly neither were bothered about Confession. Gerald wished he could be like that and not worry so much, but with so many secrets in his brain recently, he felt that there could be a strong possibility that the roof could cave in on him this time.

Aggie, Alan and Grandpa Hughes arrived punctually to join their family in the short walk to the local church. The three families all smartly dressed in their Sunday best strode out down the centre of the road to Mass. Grandpa led the way as he always did. Walking at the head of the line he proudly strode out with his daughter on the other side, his brown leather-bound prayer book tightly clasped in his hand across his chest. Gerald always found it comical to watch the adults as they walked in unison, marching like soldiers to worship a god that they couldn't see.

Thankful that the walk had not taken more than 15 minutes, Gerald swiftly made his way into the church. Doing as Alfie had proposed, he removed his tight shoes and hid them and his stocking feet under the pew. Despite being devoted churchgoers the family always chose to sit right at the back. Their reasoning was twofold, his grandpa didn't like the crowds and the ladies liked to people-watch, so they had a much better view from the rear of the church as they could see everyone come in.

The church was half-empty when they entered but the confessional row was full.

"Oh look at the queue for confession Dad!" Eileen muttered. "We won't all get in now, with that lot waiting," she groaned.

"Well it weren't long since I last went," Gerald said quickly, relieved that he had the opportunity of being dismissed from his obligations.

"You go Eileen with Grandpa, I'll look after kids," Florence smiled happily.

"Aren't you going then Florrie?" Eileen quizzed.

"Not today, Eileen no!" she replied reflectively.

"Come on then Dad, looks like it's just the two of us," she said disapprovingly as she glanced at Florence. Gerald's mother pensively watched the couple genuflect as they left the pew side and headed in the direction of the confessional rows. He wondered why his mother's head tilted downwards into a regretful bow. She never seemed to enjoy coming to church, he thought, and he assumed that she did it because his dad's family were such devout Catholics. He wondered when his mother had last gone to Confession; he had always assumed that she'd gone in the week when he was at school. He'd never seen her go on a Sunday, she had always said that it was too busy but now he questioned whether she went at all.

With Confession over, the family all huddled together on the back row in anticipation of the priest's sermon.

"I bet you he does the parable about the forbidden fruit," Eileen sniggered as she gestured towards Mrs Johnson, who was sitting bolt upright on the front row, her doting husband dutifully at her side.

"Oh I'm sure he will," Florence giggled.

"She'd have suggested it straight away no doubt, moment them apples went missing," Aggie chimed in.

"Suppose Father O'Donnell feels like he needs to keep is parishioners happy, otherwise he'd have no help, so you can't blame him," Florence pondered.

"I think... she abuses her position in the church, to get what she wants," Eileen scorned.

"What do you mean Eileen?" the two sisters echoed.

"Oh she wasn't always so righteous, I could tell you something that would knock her right off her high perch." The sisters shook their heads in unison; they knew she'd never tell.

"One for your book eh Eileen," Aggie said judgmentally. Eileen threw her a sharp look of indignation, annoyed that Aggie knew anything about her little black book. Florence, quick to detect tension growing between the two, jabbed Aggie sharply in the ribs silencing her for the rest of the service.

Gerald had been relieved to get out from the church. He had already felt hot and bothered in his tight shoes and smart clothes, but his situation had progressively worsened when the priest had pointed his finger at his congregation during his sermon, as if demanding a confession for the missing apples.

"Ooh that were horrible," Gerald confessed to Susan.

"Thought you were going to crack there for a minute," she flushed.

"No, I would never tell, promised Clive dint I, and a promise is a promise." The cousins joined by Josie, linked arms and skipped all the way back to Gerald's house. Gratefully, Gerald changed out of his Sunday best and into cooler more suitable clothing. There was no customary Sunday roast today they had another tradition to uphold.

Every first Sunday during the cousins' stay, the four aunties stopped their chores and gathered their families together at the very top field near the stream behind the

Osborne's farm. The aunties worked tirelessly baking in preparation for their annual picnic event and the siblings were never disappointed. With the exception of Uncle Vic, everyone made the journey through the tall yellow cornfield to the green meadow running alongside the stream.

This year was no exception, the elder boys would be home on annual leave and Albert would be back from London to join the family jaunt as he had every year since he'd moved up north from his southern home some 11 years before. They all looked forward to this family day, it had become a tradition. It was a special time when they could laugh without thinking, have fun without trying and relish in their large family unit. It was a hot day, the hottest they'd had all summer. Aggie had to set up the picnic and so had asked Gerald and Susan if they would take Kim for her.

"I'll see you up there later," she had nodded when they collected the boisterous dog from her house.

"Come on then girl, let's go!" Gerald laughed as he fought to control the huge dog, which stood taller than him on her hind legs. Kim enjoyed the long walks in the fields she had with Gerald, he would play fetch with her for hours and run her ragged. She loved Aggie and her devotion showed but Aggie struggled to contain the energetic dog. She religiously walked her devoted pet every day but her damaged lungs caused their walks to often be cut short.

Kim raced ahead; she was bursting with energy after being cooped up all morning while they'd been in church. When the cousins reached the top part of the field they saw Alfie and Clive already at the stream. The boys were stripped down to their shorts, their clothes and shoes strewn across the bank. They took it in turns to energetically swing back and forth across the stream on the rope swing.

"Whoooow," they screamed as they relished the game and cool water at their descent.

Kim instantly spotted the signs of fun and charged towards them, she was a lively character who was totally fearless. She wasted no time in joining in the activity; running at full speed she launched herself into the air, opened her mouth wide and stretched for the large knot tied at the end of the rope. Grasping it expertly in her jaws she swung to and fro motionless, enjoying the sheer delight of the swaying, her hind legs hanging limply as she reeled. When the rope had ceased to rock, she confidently dropped into the stream below, quickly reverting to her animated self as she splashed frantically about in the refreshing water.

"Are you having a go Susan?" Clive teased, remembering how she had landed face first in the icy water last summer. Susan was sceptical at first, but she was determined not to be the butt of her brother's jokes so she decided to give it a go.

"Go on Suze!" Alfie egged her on. "It'll be fine you'll see." Susan, cheered on by her cousins, took hold of the rope.

"OK, here goes," she said, as she jumped so that her legs wrapped tightly around the rope. "Wee!" she screamed with joy as the glorious motion and exhilarating feeling put all her fears aside.

"Your turn Gerald," Susan said as she carefully dismounted the rope. Just like Alfie and Clive, Gerald stripped down to his shorts but unlike Susan, he hurled himself at the swing and at speed dangled backwards taking in the joyful faces of his upside down cousins.

"My turn now, my turn," Josie demanded, as she watched her cousin continue to sway. Josie had arrived late, as she had elected to help carry the picnic and was determined not to be left out.

"Not be a minute Jose, just two more swings and it's all yours," Gerald said calmly. As the swing came to a standstill and his turn ended Josie eagerly took the rope in her small hands and propelled herself up into the air with real vigour; her athleticism put them all to shame.

"Push me higher!" Josie roared. The cousins applauded the little girl as she performed for them. "Bet you can't do this!" she boasted. "Watch me! Watch me!" Josie shouted turning upside down on the rough cord and then stood tall on the knot and balanced one legged with natural skill.

Soaked to the bone and hungry from their exertion, the cousins headed towards the adults that had set up camp further away from the stream. Uncle Alan had set out the cricket pitch as usual. He was in his element when it came to sports and games and thoroughly enjoyed the annual event. Dressed in his summer whites and cap, he precisely paced out the crease and distance between the wickets and proudly unpacked all of the equipment including the cricket bat and ball. Alan was a perfectionist and took great care of his belongings, keeping them in immaculate condition. Every year he produced the cricket gear unscathed, despite their annual grilling.

Everyone knew his methodical regime ensured that all the equipment was maintained. He spent hours meticulously cleaning the mud and grass from it all, rubbing the bat with linseed oil to preserve its life and proudly stowing them away safely for the next year. Both he and Aggie had been very sporty in their youth and although they lived harmoniously together day-to-day, when it came to competing in sports they came to blows. Despite her obvious frailty Alan always wanted Aggie to play on his team, she was his nemesis and he knew it.

It was tradition that the two youngest participating children always picked the teams, so that they didn't get left until last. This year, that title fell to Josie and making his debut Geoffrey, who had just turned six. Aunty Lily was proud to have another of her offspring on the team and especially pleased as he was her only boy. She had made him a black armband to mark the occasion of his first captaincy, whereas Josie was an old hand at it now, after captaining her first team the year before. Being the sportsperson that she was, Josie had remembered from the previous year, who would be best to pick. The children were keen to get started, but Alan had insisted that they wait until all candidates had arrived.

"Oh you've made it!" Florence shouted as she saw her two elder sons approaching, flanked by her two eldest daughters. Keenly she ran to greet them lovingly thrilled to have her boys' home for a couple of days. Charlie and Billy were dressed smartly in their respective military regalia, as was the expectation when they came home on leave, but they soon stripped down to their bare skins like their younger siblings as the heat penetrated through their uniforms. Florence searched the horizon for the last player and checked her watch.

"Anyone seen Albert?" she asked anxiously, but no one had an answer. The sisters gathered together around the blanketed area and helped Lily cluck over her smaller children who would not be playing that day. Aggie paid most attention to the baby, who she tenderly soothed into a deep sleep. She placed the babe in her old pram and shaded her from the sun. She looked up from the carriage and caught the watchful eye of Florence.

"You OK?" Florence mouthed, seeing her sister bravely holding in her grief.

"Yes I'm all right," she said, wiping away her tears and setting to work busying herself with the other children giving them colouring and simple games to play. "Anything to keep them entertained eh!" Aggie smiled meekly at Florence.

Eileen handed out towels to the rope swingers, dished out drinks, sandwiches and home-baked cookies to the competitors. Cricket was the ideal game for the mothers, because it meant that once a year they each got to have a well-earned break, as the batting team could take it in turns to look after the younger ones whilst they had their innings.

"Afternoon everyone," a familiar voice called, Gerald abandoned his sandwich and spun round quickly to greet the final candidate. Albert was impressively dressed in his cricket whites, but his love for colour still featured in his maroon cravat which was tied fashionably around his neck. He embraced his young chum and smiled a knowing smile.

He reached into his pocket and pulled out a farthing and excitedly said, "Shall I flip?"

"Yeh!" Josie screamed in delight as her chosen king's head gained her first pick. "Can I have Alan please," she said excitedly.

"Oh good choice little lady," he said as he ran to join her.

"I'll have me Anty Aggie please," Geoffrey said nervously. Alan was not pleased that Geoffrey had pointed to his adversary to join his team.

"Game on Alan!" Aggie chuckled as she rushed to join her nephew's side.

After five minutes the teams were chosen but they were odd, nine on Josie's and ten on Geoffrey's.

"You can be umpire, Grandpa," Florence called.

"Righto, I'll just sit here then shall I?" he said as he gestured towards the deckchair.

"Yes Dad sit there," Eileen agreed motioning him to take his seat.

"I think he's likely to fall asleep for most of match anyhow," Aggie chuckled to Gerald who was also on her team.

"What about Kim?" Susan quickly pointed out.

"I think she'll be more of hindrance than a help," Aggie replied.

"I think Anty Aggie should be allowed a runner if she needs one," Gerald shouted feeling a little concerned for his auntie's health.

"Oh I don't think that's fair!" Alan protested.

"Oh Alan don't be mardy," Eileen said, appalled by his harshness. Aggie just laughed, she knew he didn't want her to have any advantage over him than the mental one she already had.

"Better get ready to catch Al," Aggie teased. She may have had poor lungs but she was a marvellous hitter and could really whack a ball.

As Josie had won the toss for first pick, Geoffrey was given the option of batting or fielding first. His team huddled together.

"What's it going be then little man?" his Aunty Aggie asked.

Geoffrey shrugged his shoulders. "I dunt know what to choose," he said as tears welled up in his eyes.

"It's OK mate," Charlie said bending down to comfort his little cousin.

"I think we should bat first before other team start to gel," Aggie suggested. All agreed, the annual cricket match commenced; runs were scored, batters caught out, lbw's dismissed and awarded. It was family fun at its very best, no cares or worries, just laughter and innocent banter on a warm summer's afternoon.

"Oh no," Alan sighed as the over ended and Aggie stepped up to the crease to bowl.

"Don't worry I'll be gentle with you Al," Aggie teased as she blew him a kiss.

Alan smiled and shook his head and said, "Come on then woman, give me your best ball!" Alan got set to prepare himself for one of her usual high bouncing balls but she tricked him and sent him a pea-roller along the floor. He waited what seemed like an age for the ball to reach his bat. Casually he swung to knock it away in disgust but lost his footing and the leather ball trickled through the crease, hit the stumps and knocked the bails off ending his innings and the game.

"How's that?" Aggie shouted looking at grandpa for judgement, as she jumped for joy.

Grandpa snorted himself awake from the comfort of his deckchair and convincingly lifted his finger and shouted, "OUT." Aggie shimmied up to her husband, threw her arms around his neck and planted a kiss on his pursed lips. Alan eventually saw the funny side. He smiled and squeezed his wife, shook his head in disbelief and bowed out gracefully docking his cap at his talented wife. It wasn't that he was inept at the game, quite the opposite, he had already scored 20 runs, but she just had that effect on him.

"What's score then Grandpa?" Gerald asked as he raced to view his score pad.

"Despite Aggie's superb effort," he said, as he winked at Aggie, "it's a victory for Josie's team!"

"Yes!" Alan shouted with glee. "Victory is ours yet again Josie," he said as he scooped up his young captain.

"You only won because Kim fielded like a demon," Billy argued.

"I think she should get players' player of the match," Gerald laughed.

Seeing that her little boy was starting to cry, Aunty Lily stepped forward said, "And our Geoffrey should get best newcomer." They all agreed it was a good idea and that Josie got an award for sportsmanship.

"And everyone gets a bowl of strawberries and cream," Florence called from the picnic blanket.

"It's been a wonderful day hasn't it?" Albert said gently patting the top of Gerald's head as he sat down next to him.

"Yeh it as," Gerald replied.

"How's Douglas? I understand Aggie found him a safe haven," Albert whispered. Gerald thought about his friend, hidden under his auntie's bed, locked inside his cocoon. "What's wrong child?" Albert enquired affectionately. Gerald snuggled into Albert's fatherly embrace.

"He'll be sleeping soon," Gerald sobbed. "And then he'll be gone forever." Albert hugged him tightly, understanding that Douglas would be turning into a chrysalis soon.

"Take a look around you Gerald, what do you see?" Gerald thought as he watched his large, united family. He observed their raucous laughter, their playful manner, the ease of conversation and the unconditional love which flowed amongst them. He had all this and was lucky enough to have Douglas too for a short while. "As much as it hurts to lose Douglas, you've been blessed to have had time with him," Albert said thoughtfully. Gerald agreed that he was lucky in both respects.

"So Gerald would you like Douglas to return to my house with me or are you content for him to remain at your Aunty Aggie's?" Albert asked. Gerald thought about how thrilled his aunty was that he'd trusted her and he didn't want to hurt her but he knew that Douglas would be safer at Albert's now that the cousins were here.

"I'd like him to come back to yours if that's OK?" Gerald said.

"As you wish, I will come and collect him tomorrow then," Albert smiled. "I have a few errands to run first after my trip, so I won't be able to get there until late afternoon," he explained. Gerald was anxious to know where he'd been and was still a little hurt that he'd left him at all but he knew Albert would tell him when he wanted him to know, so he had to be patient.

"Come on you two," Florence beckoned; the family had packed away and declared their annual day of fun over. Albert beamed at Florence, her hair tousled down one side and her face flushed from the exercise. "Did you have a good trip?" Florence asked politely.

"It wasn't a pleasurable one, but I think things will be better soon," he sighed sadly.

Florence looked into his hazel eyes and reached for her friend's hand. Squeezing it tightly she said, "I'm here for you if you need me Albert, I know I weren't always, but I am now." Albert reciprocated her grasp and looked deep within the blue lagoons with hope in his heart.

"I know you are Florrie," he said softly, his heart aching.

"Come on Gerald," Florence called brightly as she relinquished her grip and reached out to take hold of her son's hand. "We'll see you soon then Albert?" Florence smiled hopefully as she walked away from him down towards her marital home. Albert looked up at the red summer night sky, it was like parting from someone you loved he thought; the light had turned down, but its warmth still remained. As much as he desired it, Albert knew that their love was impossible while there was possibility of Charlie still being alive. Grateful that she had allowed him back into her life so fully, he turned and made the solitary journey home alone in the hope that one day they'd know one way or another if Charlie was still alive.

Day Eight
A Pain Healed

Gerald woke at his usual time on the Monday morning and rushed to get dressed. He had slept better despite the cramped conditions in his bedroom. He chuckled to himself as he clambered over the bodies of his two brothers camping out on the floor. Yesterday had been fun he thought and he was happy to have his favourite brother home. His day had been so busy yesterday with church and all the merriment of the cricket match, he had not had chance to see Douglas. He knew that he was safe because his Aunty Aggie had confirmed as much when they were waiting to bat but Gerald was anxious to see for himself. He thundered down the stairs only to be greeted by his mum's sewing machine, which sat waiting ominously at the bottom.

"UUUH," he groaned as it dawned on him that it was Monday and that meant sewing day for his Aunty Aggie.

The sewing machine was passed between the sisters and it was Gerald's job to take it to his Aunty Aggie's. Gerald's Uncle Alan passed it on to his Aunty Lily when Aggie had finished with it and Alfie fetched it back. He didn't mind doing the errand because it was for his Aunty Aggie; it was just that it was so heavy. Eyeing the monstrosity as he passed it, Gerald's weak little arms ached at the thought of lifting the heavy contraption.

"Morning Gerald," his mum said pleasantly still cheerful from the day before.

"Morning Mam. You want me to take sewing machine up to me Anty Aggie's?" he asked gaily.

"Oh you don't have to bother today sweetheart," she beamed, "Charlie said he'd take it for you. I know it's a struggle for you."

"No I can take it Mam honest," Gerald quickly replied anxious that he would miss his opportunity to see Douglas. "I... I... could ask Suze to help me today."

"Ask Susan to do what?" Susan said as she emerged from the doorway. Susan drifted angelically into the kitchen. She was immaculately presented in a new blue dress with a white apron tied loosely in a bow around her trim waste, her blonde hair tied back in a half ponytail and secured neatly with a thick yellow ribbon.

"Help me carry sewing machine?" Gerald asked hopefully as he nodded towards the dusty lead machine sitting on the floor.

"Where are we carrying it to?" Susan asked with a deep sigh.

"Only to Anty Aggie's house!" Gerald said reassuringly.

"It's alright Susan love, Charlie said he'd do it for him today!" Florence said with her back to them.

"Please Suze, Douglas is there and I need to see him," Gerald mouthed.

"It's alright Aunty Florrie, I am happy to go. I like to see Kim anyway," Susan agreed willingly.

Convinced but confused by their anxiousness to carry out the task, Florence filled their bellies up with eggs and soldiers and sent them on their way.

"Flipping heck Gerald, however do you carry this thing on your own, it weighs a ton!" Susan grimaced, her knees buckling under the machine's weight.

"I use window ledges to rest on, when it gets too heavy," he said as he motioned towards his neighbour's ledge. The cousins were thankful as they turned the street corner into Aggie's street, until they saw her anxiously waiting in the doorway. Gerald wondered why she was looking so concerned and began to worry. The weight of the sewing machine prevented him from getting to her any quicker.

"What's up Anty Aggie?" he shouted breathlessly. Aggie stepped out of her house and hesitantly helped them carry the machine indoors. Last time she'd lifted it the consequences had been drastic. "What's wrong?" Gerald asked again, beginning to panic now. "Are you OK?"

"I'm all right just feel a tad faint, nowt to worry your head about," replied Aggie.

Sure that she was OK Gerald asked, "Is it Douglas? Has summat happened to Douglas?" His Aunty Aggie sat down to catch her breath, she was breathing heavily from her exertion.

"You'd better go and see for your sen!"

"You go Gerald," Susan gestured. "I'll stay here and see to Aggie." Gerald raced up the stairs, devotedly followed by Kim. Hesitantly he pushed open his auntie's bedroom door, unsure of what he would find. Maybe Douglas has changed, he considered wistfully to himself. Perhaps his bright green eyes were no longer shining, or possibly his fur no longer glistened, could his foot be conceivably no longer shoeless? Satisfied that everything was as it had been, he quickly fell on his knees to the floor and shoved back the bed frame. Unsure what he expected to see, he carefully pulled the floorboard away from the space that Douglas had been placed in and peered inside. Whatever he'd imagined, nothing could prepare the little boy for what he saw. Douglas was gone!

Gerald searched frantically under the floorboard for his companion but he could see no sign. He looked again for him in the box, but all that remained were the green leaves he had munched on and a strange ridged bean-like stone that Gerald didn't recognise. He lay motionless next to his friend's empty box, he felt a strange pain inside his chest and tears began to run like rivers from his eyes. Douglas had been his friend, he couldn't understand where or why he'd gone, he'd not even had a chance to say goodbye. Wherever he was, he hoped that he knew that his heart was breaking without him.

Kim pushed her way under the bed to snuggle in by Gerald's side and sniffed inquisitively at the box.

"He's gone girl," Gerald sobbed as he stroked his canine companion.

"Who's gone?" Susan said as her head appeared at the side of the bed.

"Douglas, he's not in box," he lifted the box out of the hiding place and pushed it towards Susan. She took the wooden receptacle from her tearful cousin and examined its contents.

"He's still in here Gerald, he's just sleeping that's all," she said comfortingly. Gerald wiped his sodden face with his woollen tank top and together with Kim, hauled himself out from under the bed.

"What do you mean? I can't see him!" he sniffed. Susan reached inside the box and lifted out the stone-like object.

"He's a chrysalis now, and he'll be like this for the next seven days, like I told you he would," she reassured him.

Gerald had never seen a chrysalis before and he marvelled at the texture of Douglas' new form. He'd lost track of the days because of the goings-on and had forgotten that Susan had told him this would happen.

"Can I have him?" Gerald said as he reached out to take the cocoon from his cousin.

"Don't worry he's still in there," Susan said as she passed him over. Lovingly, Gerald ran his fingertips over the rough exterior, just as he had stroked Douglas' fur only a few days before. There was no purring coming from the creature today, but Gerald was sure the object was getting warmer as he caressed his friend.

Gerald exhaled deeply, he felt drained, he'd never felt such sorrow and emotion since Douglas had come into his life and it was beginning to take its toll on him.

"You OK Gerald?" Susan said as she looped her arm around his shoulder.

"Just want expecting it that's all Suze!" Gerald said glancing into her beautiful blue eyes.

"Come on, I think you're a bit tired from carrying that flaming machine," Susan soothed as she reached out to take Gerald's hand.

"I just want to be with him for a little bit do you think me Anty Aggie would mind me lying on her bed?" Gerald gestured.

"No I'm sure she'll be fine with it," Susan said tapping the bed's patchwork blanket. Gerald took the outstretched hand of his cousin and heaved his small frame up off the floor to perch on the edge of his auntie's bed. "I'll just go and check on Aggie and come back up in a while, OK?" Susan reassured him.

Gerald gently cupped Douglas in a loving embrace and closed his eyes tightly to block out the hurt.

"I thought I'd lost you," he said as he stared down at an object that he didn't know. He longed to see the quirky face of the caterpillar smiling back at him. Although he understood that he was a caterpillar and that it was natural for him to change, he didn't see that it would necessarily be true for Douglas if he was truly magical. There had to be a reason that he was now encased in this cocoon state, he only wished that he could work it out.

Gerald rolled back on to his auntie's bed and held the chrysalis up high to examine it more carefully. Remembering his experience at Albert's house, Gerald closed his eyes tightly and waited for the images to drift into his mind. It had been exhausting to experience the flashbacks but Gerald desired it more than ever, now that Douglas was no longer visible and so allowed himself to relax in a deep sleep.

Confident that Aggie had fully recovered, Susan made her way back up the stairs to check on her cousin. Seeing that he had fallen asleep and believing that it must have been the shock, Susan felt it best to leave him again for a short while. She searched inside the chest of drawers for something to cover him while he slept and found a white crocheted blanket. Motherly, she laid it across him, the small blanket just covering his shoulders and hiding the encasement in his hands.

"Come on Kim," she said as she dragged the reluctant dog out from under the bed. Quietly she vacated the room leaving her cousin to sleep for a while.

Comforted by the warmth emanating from Douglas and the small treasured blanket, Gerald eased into a resting sleep, which enabled moments from the past to once again flood into his dreams. The images were hazy at first, but Gerald could make out the same couple he had seen in a previous image, but this time the memory went further back. It was a time before they had their child, as the woman was heavily pregnant. They stood looking at the sorrowful face of a younger woman her expression sharpened the perspective. She held in her hand a white crocheted blanket and knelt at the foot of a tiny crib, her grief was laden with guilt. The lady looked tortured and in his dream Gerald felt an overwhelming urge to reach out and comfort her.

The image of the woman faded slowly and it was replaced with the smiling face of a handsome man, who was holding a baby girl in his arms. The voice that Gerald had heard before was speaking now, like a running commentary over the images, giving assurances that her mortal life had never meant to be. It was no one's fault that her life had lasted no more than a few moments. The sense that the baby had been too weak to thrive was overwhelming. She was small and weak but she was safe and secure now in her angel's protective grasp.

The whispers died away and Gerald felt himself being swayed back and forth, a voice clear, soft and gentle stirring him out of his slumber. He awoke to see the beautiful tear-filled eyes of his dreams staring back at him. Aggie thoughtfully stroked his shoulders where the precious blanket secured his warmth.

"Oh Anty Aggie," he said as he rose to comfort her just as he wished he could have in his dreams.

"What did I do to deserve this?" Aggie asked still wrapped in Gerald's soft embrace.

"It isn't from me," he replied kindly, "I think it's from your little girl."

Gerald slowly withdrew from his auntie's tender hold. Sure that the vision would come again he placed the warm casket of Douglas in his auntie's hands. Aggie looked bemused at Gerald. "Trust me, you need to feel this Anty!" he said placing his small hand over hers. She wasn't a spiritual person and didn't really believe in an afterlife, her grieving just seemed to last forever. She tried to comprehend how Gerald knew that the child she'd lost was a girl, she knew he'd seen the baby clothes, but they were not gender specific and the shawl had been white and the tag not bearing her chosen first name.

"Just close your eyes, Douglas will do rest!" Gerald said as he traded places with his aunty. The disbeliever held the strange bean-like shape in her hands and closed her eyes as she was instructed. The darkness behind her lids slowly disappeared leaving behind a misty hue. The warmth from the encased creature flowed gently through her body and she wept as the image of her child safe and secure in the arms of an angel appeared. She was saddened, as she felt her daughter's weakness and began to understand why she hadn't lived. The image lasted only a few moments and then faded from her sight. Slowly she opened her eyes and raised herself up.

"I thought he were special Gerald," she said as she caressed the cocoon in her hands. "But I dint know he were magical till now." Tearfully she handed Douglas back to her young nephew and smiled. "Thank you," she said, "for sharing your special gift with me Gerald, I feel like he's set me free."

"What happened to your baby?" Gerald asked. Aggie shuffled back to the top of her bed and snuggled underneath her warm blanket and looked directly at Gerald.

"For years I've not been able to talk about losing her, it were too raw for a long time." Aggie glanced at the cocoon held in Gerald's grasp and smiled, "But now I know she's with angels, I feel ready." Gerald placed Douglas back in his casket underneath the bed and crawled into the vacant space in the bed next to his aunty.

She snuggled him tightly and began her story. "Well you know that monstrosity that you lugged over here today?"

"Yeh!" Gerald replied, still aching from carrying its weight.

"Well I fell trying to carry it," she sighed.

"When you was pregnant?" Gerald gasped.

"Yeh," Aggie nodded. "19 weeks."

"Why dint someone offer to carry it for you?" he said, annoyed that they hadn't.

"Oh they did! Billy brought it to door, but like you he weren't a very big lad then and so out of sympathy I told him to leave it and his Uncle Alan would fetch it me in later."

Gerald looked reproachfully at his aunty and said, "You dint wait did you?"

"No Gerald, I dint. I were stupid, naïve and impatient and thought I could do it me sen," Aggie said shamefully.

"Oh Aggie," Gerald said as he squeezed her tight.

"The next day I started to bleed and it wouldn't stop. I dint want to go to hospital again, I'd had enough after being in with me TB, but bleeding were awful," she winced. "Huge amounts, so in end I had no choice. Everyday were a bonus, because it meant pregnancy wouldn't be viable if babe came early," Aggie said as she stroked her empty belly. "After nearly five weeks in hospital, they moved me to bigger hospital," she said nodding in the direction of the city. "Said it were best option for premature babies, but I were frightened and dint want to go," Aggie said showing Gerald the fear in her eyes. "I've always known when summat's not right with me health and I guess I knew in me heart that she weren't going to make it," she said stroking Gerald's hair. "And I were right, she died same day."

"Doctors said that all the blood loss nearly cost me my life, but I dint care because I just wanted to die too. We struggled to find her a name and because hope was all that we had left to hold on to, we called her that."

"Did you have a funeral?" Gerald asked as he shivered at the thought.

"No ducky, state took care of it for me, wasn't strong enough to cope with it at time," replied Aggie. Gerald understood her reluctance to bury her baby. He had been terrified when Clive had trapped him into the deep dark hole last summer. The thought of a tiny baby in such a pit horrified him. He could see as she spoke, that Aggie had regrets that she never gave her little girl a proper burial.

"Do you know what they did with her body Anty Aggie?" Gerald asked kindly.

"No just walked away and left her there," she said shamefully. "Later, when I felt stronger, I felt disgusted with me sen for doing that but I never felt brave enough to find out. Thought they'd judge me, see."

Gerald raised his head to look into his auntie's eyes. "Would you like me to help you find her Anty Aggie?" he offered brightly.

"Oh Gerald, that's right kind of you lad but I think it's something that your Uncle Alan and I need to do together," she said as she squeezed him tightly. Gerald squeezed her back affectionately feeling saddened that she had suffered all these years, wallowing silently in her own grief and hiding her misery behind her laughter.

"Can I come in?" Susan asked as she peered through the door.

"Yes duck," Aggie said apologetically as she wiped the tears from her eyes.

"Is everything alright?" Susan asked concerned.

"Everything's going to be a lot better than it has been for past ten years!" Aggie said, as she threw back the blanket and straightened out her dress.

"Ten years?" Gerald said thoughtfully.

"Yes, duck, your Mam and me were pregnant at same time but mine want to be," she said sadly. "Your Mam were heartbroken that her little sister had lost her first baby and I suspect a little guilty because she'd already had five strong healthy children," Aggie sighed thoughtfully.

"Dint you ever want to try for another baby Anty Aggie?" Gerald mused.

"We did," she breathed. "Lost them really early on too, guess it weren't meant to be." Gerald studied his auntie's regretful expression and wondered whether she blamed herself for the death of her first and only child.

"You were a gift ta your Mam and Dad," she said brightly as she wiped the tears away from her eyes. "They had a rough patch for a while, then you came along and it sempt to bring them back together." Gerald smiled as he realised that the image he saw in his dream was of his parents. "Your Dad was a tower of strength to me and ya Uncle Alan. Tretted me like I were his little sister too. Dunt think I could have got through it without him," she explained. He thought of the image of the man holding her baby and wondered if it was his dad holding the baby in his arms. If it was, he sadly thought that he too must be dead.

"Suppose she'll be with our David now," she beamed, happy that she'd seen her baby encased in the arms of an angel.

"Who's David?" Gerald asked confused.

"He's your Aunty Aggie's twin, isn't he Aggie?" Susan chirped seizing the chance to be part of this deep conversation.

"Yeh he died when you two were very young," Aggie said regretfully. "He caught pneumonia." Gerald thought hard about the image of the handsome man and wondered whether it could be David instead of his father. If that was so, there was still hope that his dad was still alive.

When Uncle Alan came home, Susan and Gerald left Aggie's house with the promise that when Aggie found where Hope was buried, they'd help her plant a rose tree in her memory. Aggie had said as it was the anniversary soon and she would like to do it then if she could. Gerald could see that his Uncle Alan was relieved that Aggie now saw it as a celebration of her daughter's birth and Gerald began to understand why his uncle had become so estranged in the past. They'd shared an experience that they would never forget and one which no one would believe. He was glad that he'd shared his secret with his Aunty Aggie, she'd not only found a solution to his problem like she said she would but she'd started to heal her own scars in the process.

The cousins walked silently on the short journey to Gerald's house and were welcomed heartily into the busy family home. The huge family crammed around the kitchen table for their late lunch, Gerald glanced around the table at his siblings and Albert's words flooded into his mind. He'd come to realise today how lonely life could be without family and he realised that Albert and Aggie lived without the joy of children living in their homes and for the first time he understood how truly lucky he was.

As the evening drew in, Gerald opted to go to bed early, aware that if he didn't, he would lose his bed for the night. He thought about Albert as he snuggled down to sleep. Albert hadn't come to Aggie's house that day, like he said he would and much to Florence's disappointment, he did not visit her either throughout the evening. Gerald wondered where he could be, he was behaving very mysteriously of late and he didn't know why. He'd heard him talk to his mother at the cricket match and so knew that his trip had not been a pleasant one. He felt concerned that as his trip was to London, he wondered whether his friends James and Michael were OK. He still missed their company and he'd always have a special place in his heart for them, but he thought about his first week of summer and how amazing it had been and realised that it was the first time since they'd left that he'd not felt lost and alone.

Day Nine
Canine Capers

The return of Charlie and Billy meant that the boys' bedroom was bursting at the seams with five young men cramped into the small bedroom. It hadn't mattered so much last year, as only Charlie had made it back in time for the annual cricket match; Billy had got called up for national service and was doing his basic training. The other children had been much smaller then and in the last 12 months they had grown considerably. After two sleepless nights it was suggested that someone would need to be billeted out.

"Mam I think we should get home comforts, as we're only here for a bit," Charlie argued.

"I tend to agree with older lads," Florence said nodding her head.

"Would we go to Anty Aggie's house?" Gerald asked hopefully.

"Yes Gerald, I asked her tuther day if she'd be willing to take on more lodgers."

"I don't mind going Mam," Gerald said instantly.

"Good lad," Florence beamed. She wasn't at all surprised, as she knew his fondness for his aunty. Pleased that the decision wasn't entirely hers she looked apprehensively towards Alfie and Clive.

"I'm definitely not going!" Alfie squirmed.

"Oh Alf you can't still be afraid of the dog!" Billy teased.

"He is..." Clive laughed. "Wets his pants every time he sees her."

Florence turned and glared at Clive. "As you're such a big brave boy Clive, you can go too," she shouted.

"I don't mind," Clive retorted pretending not to care, but he didn't look too pleased that he was going to stay at Aggie's as well.

"That's settled then!" she said smiling triumphantly. "Gerald, nip round to your Anty Aggie's and tell her whose coming will you?" Florence said kindly. She knew Aggie would be pleased that Gerald was coming, but would not be so keen on Clive, so she felt that she should be forewarned.

"Yeh, all right Mam," Gerald said happily and he quickly sped off to gather together a few belongings before heading swiftly to his auntie's house.

"Oh for goodness' sake," Aggie exclaimed, as Gerald delivered the news. "It had to be him dint it, the little weasel," she said shaking her head.

"We need a plan Anty Aggie, what if he finds Douglas?" Gerald said anxiously.

"We'll not let that happen lad, anyway he'll not try it on this time," she said confidently.

"How can you be so sure?" Gerald asked.

"Last summer, I caught him riffling through me stuff and I caught him stealing me money," Aggie replied.

"What did you say when you caught him?" Gerald gasped.

"Let's just say, unless he's got a very short memory, he'll not want to be doing naughty things under my roof," she said firmly as she folded her arms. Aggie wasn't one to stir up trouble and she hadn't said anything to his mother, as she knew Eileen didn't take kindly to people accusing her children. Aggie was wise enough to avoid the wrath of Eileen and her vengeful letters; she'd seen the damage she could do with those.

Aggie put Gerald's belongings in the room he was to share with his grandpa. She fastened a sheet on some string and fixed it down the middle, to give the old man some privacy.

"What's that for?" Gerald asked bemused.

"Grandpa not take kindly to sharing with Clive," Aggie grimaced at Gerald, "And we don't want to upset is mood do we?" Grandpa didn't like Clive either, he just grunted at him when he saw him, he thought Eileen had spoilt him. Aggie, happy that Grandpa would be pleased with her efforts, trundled out of the room.

As they made their way out, Gerald glanced casually at his aunt's bedroom next door to his and sighed.

Seeing her nephew's concern, Aggie cradled his shoulder with her arm and drew him in close and said, "Don't worry about Douglas, we'll just have to be extra careful, while Clive's here Gerald, OK."

"Hopefully Albert will collect Douglas today and then we'll not have to worry," Gerald replied as they made their way down the stairs.

"In meantime keep him out of house. Tell you what, take our Kim for walk up in fields and make sure Clive goes with you," Aggie said wagging her finger in the air.

"I'll stay out for as long as I can Anty Aggie," Gerald agreed as he grabbed the dog's lead off its hook and slipped it on to her collar. "Tell Albert I'll visit him later if I miss him OK!" Gerald said as he frantically raced from the doorway.

"Back already!" Susan and Josie chimed simultaneously, as Gerald arrived back at his house.

"Yeh thought we could go out for a bit of a walk, dint want to get under me Anty Aggie's feet," he said as he nodded towards Clive. Susan stared at Gerald quizzically but then she smirked when she realised that he was just keen to keep Clive away from Douglas.

"What are you laughing at?" Josie said annoyed that she wasn't in on the joke.

"Nothing, it doesn't matter," Susan said shuffling the little girl out of the door. Eager to get out into the fresh air, Kim boisterously pushed passed Josie nearly knocking her over.

"Steady Kim," Gerald yelped as he strove to hold on to the big dog's lead.

"Come on Kim, I'll hold your lead," Josie said defiantly, as she snatched her leash from Gerald's grasp.

"I don't think that's such a good idea Jose!" Gerald said concerned.

"I'm fine," Josie said undeterred and strolled on ahead.

The sanctuary of the village and the nature of their surroundings led the children to feel safe to roam wherever they pleased. The villagers smiled at the children's playful antics and only the unforgiving few saw menace in their capers. Josie had been coming to these North Nottinghamshire hills all her young life and knew them well, and so felt confident striding on ahead, but Header Vale Farm, which had always embraced the children's visits, was now farmed by Mr Osbourne, and he was less welcoming.

Susan smiled brightly at Gerald as she observed him watching Josie running comically to keep up with the huge dog.

"She'll be OK Gerald, she's tougher than she looks," Susan laughed.

"I'm not so sure, Kim can be a bit lively at times you know," Gerald replied, unable to contain his laughter.

"I'll go and get the boys and then we can catch her up," Susan suggested.

"Best hurry up before she does herself a mischief," he called after her. Susan smiled as she ran into the house in search of the bigger boys. She was pleased to see that Gerald's long rest yesterday had restored him to his usual self. She desperately wanted to ask what else he'd been talking to his Aunty Aggie about before she came into the bedroom but she knew him well enough to know that if he wanted her to know he would tell her.

"Come on then let's go," Clive yelled as he and Alfie rushed out of the door in search of the youngest sibling. With the two boys' safe by their sides, the four wily cousins raced to catch Josie, who was by now so far ahead she was almost out of sight. Kim had surged ahead, despite her paws aching from yesterday's frolics and Josie, who had tethered herself to the frantic dog, was grittily holding on for dear life. Kim loved the open fields, the wonderful things she could see and delicious things she could smell. It sent her crazy with excitement.

"Calm down Kim," Josie begged, as she pulled herself up off the ground for the fifth time, but Kim wanted to chase the butterflies, jump up and nip at the long rye grass, so there was no holding her back, she was relentless. Despite her determination, Josie began to tire from clinging on to the huge dog and in exhaustion the worn leather slipped through her small fingers, releasing Kim from her grasp.

"Quick, Kim's loose!" Gerald shouted as he spotted Kim free herself from Josie's small hands. The dawdling cousins ran breathlessly towards her, but it was too late Kim sprinted off leaving the fast approaching children in her wake.

"You alright Josie?" Susan asked picking the little girl up off the ground.

"Yes, I'm alright," she replied rubbing her knee. "Just bumped my knee a bit when she pulled me over," she winced.

"Told you it weren't a good idea," Gerald said knowingly.

"Sorry Gerald, I should have listened," Josie sobbed.

"It's OK no harm done, she's just playing," he said stroking the top of her head.

"I wouldn't be too sure," Alfie said in a frightened voice. The children stopped laughing as they noticed that the crazy dog had ceased playing and was staring fixedly ahead of her. Kim's head extended tall out of her neck, her tail stiff and purposeful. The hair on the back of her neck stood up and her nose poised, as if sniffing out an unfamiliar smell. Gerald couldn't understand Kim's peculiar stance; he'd seen her stalk things in the past, like she was a lion hunting her prey, but this was strange.

He looked around the fields, scouring them, trying to locate her obsession.

"As she heard summat?" Gerald quizzed Susan.

"I don't think so," Susan replied.

"Oh no!" Alfie said terrified.

"What is it? What you seen Alf?" Gerald asked frantically looking around the fields to see what Alfie had spotted. Alfie said nothing, he just pointed in the direction of the Osbourne's field. Gerald looked in the direction that Kim was headed and in the distance he could see the object of Kim's desire. Grazing contentedly in the Osbourne's pasture were six black bullocks and Kim was getting ready to sprint towards them.

"No Kim. No, no, no!" Gerald yelled frantically at the top of his voice as he raced towards her, but Kim was transfixed. "Come on we've got to stop her," Gerald shouted as he beckoned his cousins to join him.

"I'm not going," Alfie blurted, starting to cry. He was already afraid of Kim, let alone the bullocks.

"Oh if you're going to cry Alf, you'd better go and fetch some help," Clive scorned as he raced alongside Gerald in pursuit of Kim.

Alfie, thankful for his escape, ran quickly down the hill away from the action.

"It's all my fault Susan!" Josie said still whimpering. "Mummy will be really mad at me." Susan opened her arms to her little sister who fell into her embrace.

"Don't worry sweetheart, I won't let you get into trouble, it's not your fault," Susan said as she cuddled her tightly.

"Come on girls," Gerald yelled. "We need your help!" The girls reluctantly raced to catch up with the boys, who were almost at the Osbourne's field and watched in horror as Kim skilfully bounded over the fence towards the bullocks. Kim skidded to a halt. Panting loudly and wagging her tail wildly, she stood still and eyed the bullocks excitedly. When her mere presence did not provoke a reaction, she ran to the rear end of the bulls and playfully began nipping at the back of their heels to gain their attention. The bullocks were not impressed with Kim and it showed. Instinctively their innate aggression rose as they felt the need to defend themselves and their bodies turned naturally to face their attacker.

One by one the bullocks fixed their eyes on Kim and glared angrily at her. In unison they began to rhythmically paw the earth beneath their hooves

"Rrrrrumph... Rrrrrrummph," the bullocks roared sweating profusely in the intense summer heat. They snorted loudly through their shiny black flared nostrils.

"We've got to do something or else they'll kill her," Clive shouted, as he observed the bullocks' oversized heads move slowly down towards their chests as they were getting ready to charge.

"Let's scream at them, loud as we can," Susan exclaimed. "They'll be less likely to attack if they are afraid," she said confidently. The children screamed loud enough to make their throats bleed but the bullocks were not deterred. "Try throwing something at them," Susan commanded.

"Like what?" the boys retaliated.

"Take your jumpers off, shoes anything to distract them." The children were starting to feel desperate now, they could see how angry the calves were getting and Kim was in a frenzy barking and snapping at their heels. The children were hysterical, as Kim showed no signs of relinquishing her game. She had created pandemonium and the only one who was not disturbed by it all was Kim. It was purely and simply a game to her and she couldn't understand why they wanted her to stop, she was enjoying herself immensely.

In the distance they could see someone coming, they hoped it was someone who could help.

"It's Mummy," Josie yelled excitedly and Clive groaned. Eileen was sprinting up the hill with Alfie lagging behind, she was fiercely protective of her kids and their safety was all that mattered. "She's got Uncle Alan's cricket bat," Josie chirruped on.

"It's OK kids, stand back, we'll have her out of here in a jiffy," Eileen said breathlessly. Wasting no time at all Eileen climbed calmly through the wooden fence, keeping her back pressed firmly against it she stepped confidently into the bullocks' domain moving slowly towards Kim. Eileen quickly spotted Kim's lead, still trailing on the ground. Carefully she picked up the handle. "Kim," she whispered to gain her attention, but Kim didn't even flinch. "Kim," she whispered a little louder and tugged lightly on her lead. Kim craned her neck slowly to where the tugging was coming from. When she saw Eileen squatting down, attached to the other end, she growled fiercely, baring all of her teeth. Eileen, not pleased that Kim was resisting, tugged harder on the lead. "Come on Kim, don't be stubborn!" her voice a little firmer than before.

"Grrrrrrrr," Kim growled indignantly and turned back to observe the bulls.

Eileen sat back on her haunches and placed her hands on her head in exasperation, she'd run out of ideas.

"It's OK girl," came a young boy's voice. Eileen looked round astonished and saw a terrified Gerald standing by her side. "Come to me Kimmy," Gerald cooed in a wobbly voice, holding Kim's favourite titbit in his outstretched hand. Without hesitation, Kim obediently softened and ran loyally to Gerald. Eileen, amazed at the young boy's bravery, quickly handed the leash to Gerald and sent the pair steadily back towards the fence.

"Are you through?" Eileen asked, with her eyes glued to the movements of her possible assailants.

"Yeh we're safe," Gerald replied. The biggest of the bullocks had noticed Eileen's entry to the paddock and was watching her keenly as she started to slowly retreat towards the fence.

"You need to get out Mummy!" Josie screamed as she saw the angry calf moving intently towards her mother.

"It's OK sweetheart," Eileen whispered waving her hand gently at her daughter.

"No Mummy! You need to get out now!" Josie screamed again clinging desperately on to the fence.

With her eyes firmly fixed on the bull, Eileen cleared her throat and in a stern voice she said, "Josie I need you to stay calm baby OK. Mummy's going to be alright. Suze, take your sister away from the fence!" Susan immediately did as she was bid and removed the distraught child from the arena.

Satisfied that Josie's hysterics were contained, Eileen considered what her next move should be. The young bull's gaze was set on her now and he was moving purposefully towards her. She knew that the animal would be too smart to outwit and she doubted that she'd get through the fence safely any more as he was far too close. Eileen clenched the cricket bat in her hand and began to shake with fear. She knew what she could do to secure her safety, but at this moment in time it seemed a ludicrous option to attack the bull and she doubted that she'd be brave enough to do it.

Eileen had always been hopeful that she could get through the fence without a fight, but as she timidly made her way rearward towards the fence the choice was taken from her. She had successfully avoided the steaming cowpats on her way into the paddock, but as she walked steadily backwards her eye was not so keen. Eileen's open-toed sandals sunk deep within the soft muck. With a yelp of panic she mightily tugged her foot free, leaving her sandal behind. The momentum catapulted her forwards towards the bullock, which launched the cricket bat into the air and came crashing down fiercely straight across the bridge of the animal's nose.

Although the bullock was stunned and recoiled momentarily, Eileen feared his reaction and so when she had steadied herself she raised the bat again and launched a second shot, as hard as she possibly could, directly across his muzzle. Eileen fell backwards with the force of the shot and landed bottom first into the stinky poo.

"RUN MUM, RUN!" Clive shouted. On hearing Clive's screams, Eileen scrambled to her feet and ran as fast as she could barefoot over the fence to safety.

Eileen collapsed into the arms of the cheering children.

"You were amazing Mum," Clive said unable to comprehend what he had just witnessed.

"Are you alright Mummy? You were very brave," Josie said gently stroking her mum's arm.

"Yes sweetheart I am now," Eileen laughed pulling her into a loving embrace.

"Poo, you're a bit stinky," Josie recoiled. Eileen twisted round and examined the back of her previously gleaming white trousers.

"Yuck, Mum you've got poo everywhere!" Clive chimed in. Susan came in close to see the mess too, but her stomach wasn't as strong as all the rest and within seconds she'd violently vomited all over her mother's trousers.

"Aaaah Susan!" Eileen winced. "Thanks for that!"

"I'm sorry, I couldn't help it," Susan said beginning to cry. "It was the awful smell it got right under my nose." Eileen went to comfort her eldest child but then thought better of it as she didn't want a repeat performance from Susan.

"Just hold your nose, like this," Eileen said demonstrating the required action.

"What about your sandal Mummy?" Josie asked pointing through the fence at the steaming shoe.

"I think we'll leave it there Josie, unless you want to fetch it Susan?" Eileen laughed.

"No!" Susan crowed nasally, still pinching her nose.

Eileen lifted herself off the ground, took her daughters hand in hers and looked towards the fence, where the bullocks once again stood peacefully grazing.

"Come on kids, let's go home!" Eileen said still laughing hysterically.

"How did you know to hit him on nose Anty Eileen?" Gerald asked as they made their way down the hill and away from the paddock.

"Your Uncle Alan did a similar thing, years ago when we went camping!" she laughed hysterically remembering the day clearly.

"Did he use his cricket bat too Mum?" Susan asked. Eileen lifted the bat, which was still tightly gripped to her hand and examined the huge dent now lodged into its edge.

"No and he didn't fall in any poo either! I don't think Uncle Alan's going to be very pleased when he unwraps this next year, do you ?"

"No!" they chorused.

"You were very brave back there, Gerald!" Eileen said.

"Thanks," he said shyly still reeling in the terrible thoughts of what could have been.

"What about the farmer? Do you think we should say something? He's bound to know something's happened when he sees your sandal," Susan asked keeping a safe distance from her mother's stench.

"I'll go and see him later and explain," Eileen reassured her. "But for now let's just rejoice in the relief that we are all in one piece."

"Three cheers for Mummy and Gerald!" Josie shouted.

"Hip hip hooray. Hip hip hooray. Hip hip hooray!" the family cheered as they skipped down the hill hand in hand, laughing at the ludicrousness of Kim's capers, Eileen's soiled trousers and Susan delicate stomach. Gerald grinned as they bounded down the hill, for the first time he felt really accepted and he wanted to share his newfound joy with someone.

As the group reached the bottom, they saw Aggie waiting anxiously in the doorway. She had been concerned when Eileen had whipped Alan's cricket bat from its storage case and not explained why.

"What's going on Eileen?" Aggie asked as they reached her front step. "And what's that smell?" she said raising her hand to her cover her nose.

"It's OK Aggie," Eileen said as she handed over the dented bat. "The smell is me I am afraid; little mishap with a cowpat!" she said shrugging her shoulders. "I'll leave Gerald to explain the rest to you, need to change my clothes and have a bath pronto."

"I think that would be a very good idea!" Aggie said waving the smell away from under her nose. "What happened to the bat?" Aggie asked Gerald, as she turned it over in her hands.

"Kim got a bit out of control," Gerald said squirming uncomfortably as he made his way into her house.

"Why what's she done this time?" she said examining the huge indentation on the edge of the bat. Gerald guided an exhausted Kim towards her bed, unhooked her from her lead and steadily unfolded the story of the morning's events.

"Well I'm glad to hear that you're all OK. I were worried sick when Eileen raced in and took cricket bat," she said as she stowed the bat out of Uncle Alan's sight and examined her dog for damage. Gerald couldn't help feeling sad that his aunty hadn't acknowledged his braveness when he'd told her what he'd done but understood that she was just relieved to have the things she cared about so dearly, safe and unharmed. Feeling despondent, Gerald made his way up the stairs in the hope that he'd find some solace with Douglas.

When he reached his auntie's bedroom, he withdrew his companion from his secret hiding place and he held him close, waiting for the warmth to come. The heat did not penetrate through his fingertips, like it had before; there was no comforting glow from the outer shell. As he held him in his hands the coolness grew, until it was like holding an icy stone. Gerald began to shiver at first as he held the cocoon and then like waves in the sea forceful rigors of penetrating cold began to run through his body. His teeth chattered uncontrollably and his body trembled violently.

Afraid for the second time that day, he tried to release Douglas from his grasp but he couldn't feel his fingers and he was unable to part himself from this unwanted feeling. He closed his eyes and breathed slowly trying to control the shivers but they would not relent. Exhausted he once again lay back on to the warm blankets of his auntie's bed and rested there in a daze, the coldness so unwelcome. Gerald could take the intensity no longer and faded into a deep sleep, his mind once again drifting to a place he didn't know.

In his cloudy dream he saw the images of men lined up side by side in their clinical metal-framed white beds. Gerald squinted to see who they were but the men were faceless. The vision closed in on a man badly injured encased in blood-stained sheets and although he did not speak, Gerald had an alarming feeling that he was someone he knew. As Gerald stood watching from the foot of the man's bed he felt such love emanate towards him, he could feel this man's pain physically and emotionally.

Thankfully the man was not alone, he had by his side a person grieving but Gerald could not sense how they were feeling. The dream died away quickly revealing nothing more and the coldness died with it. Gerald awoke feeling confused and sad, he didn't understand the images that he was getting from Douglas and he was beginning to feel frustrated. Gerald looked at the wall clock in his auntie's room and wondered where Albert could be, he needed him now more than ever.

Gerald rose from the soft bed and gently replaced Douglas back in his safe haven. He looked at his friend encased in his tomb and wondered if he'd ever see his face again. Saddened by the thought that he may not, Gerald slid back the plank of wood, pulled back the bed frame, vacated the room and ventured down the stairs.

"Everything OK Gerald?" his Aunty Aggie asked.

"Yes," Gerald lied, "everything's fine." The day had been so eventful that Gerald felt exhausted; he wanted to share his experience with his aunty as they had done the day before but she looked worn to a crisp and he didn't want to ail her further.

Alone with his thoughts, Gerald ventured out into the backyard and withdrawing some chalk from his pocket, drew upon the concrete tiles the eight squares which made up a hopscotch game. Susan had taught him this game last summer and although he knew it wasn't really a boy's game he loved it. After spotting a perfect stone lying on the ground, Gerald happily passed the time away, while he reflected on what he'd seen, until it was time for supper.

"Dinner Gerald," Aggie said as she peeped her head around the back door.

"What we got?" Gerald asked.

"Sausage and mash and jelly and blancmange for desert," she said enthusiastically rubbing her belly.

"Great!" Gerald replied quietly.

"Is everything alright, Gerald?" Aggie asked concerned. Gerald sloshed some rainwater to wash away his hopscotch before his Uncle Alan came home and looked thoughtfully at his aunty.

"Just been a big day that's all," Gerald said as he lifted his head to meet her gaze. "Are you OK Anty Aggie?" Gerald said gently noticing that she still looked a little peaky.

"Think I'll have to go to docs if I get much worse, felt yucky for days now," she replied. "But I'll be right."

After supper Gerald stayed at his Aunty Aggie's house, he was in too solemn a mood to be with the cousins and he didn't want to miss Albert's arrival. Gerald pulled up the old red painted table, which Grandpa sometimes took his lunch on and dealt out the dominoes.

"Oh fabulous boy," Grandpa said delighted to have Gerald to pass the time with. "Used to play dominoes with your dad years ago," Grandpa beamed, as he lined up his black tiles in a semicircle out of view.

"Grandpa?" Gerald said as he placed down the double six. "Do you think me dad's still alive, Grandpa?" Grandpa Hughes bent his head down towards his hands and shook his head gently from side to side.

"He's been gone an awful long time now lad," he replied doubtfully.

"I know but do you think that maybe there's even a chance he could be?" Gerald asked hopefully.

"Anything's possible son," he said meekly as he slipped his middle finger on the inside of his glasses to remove a tear. Gerald could see how upset it made his grandpa to talk about his missing son and so respectfully he didn't broach the subject again.

Laughter was restored later that evening when his Uncle Alan had returned from work and he and Aggie joined them in a game of cards. Gerald noticed how caring and attentive his uncle was to his aunt now and wondered what had changed his character. Aggie had relayed Kim's capers to him when he got home and Alan had surprisingly laughed when he'd seen the damaged cricket bat.

"Me Anty Eileen said she got idea from you Uncle Alan, on a camping trip," Gerald said.

"Did Eileen tell you why?" Alan said looking mischievously at Aggie.

"No why, what happened?" Gerald pressed.

"Well," he said as he pulled Aggie's hand away from shielding her face. "Aggie got caught short in middle of night and wandered into field, not realising it were occupied," he laughed as he recounted the story. "She just froze when she heard them," he said grinning at Aggie. "I heard her go for a wee and I knew that she were still a little bit tipsy, so I went to find her and there she were standing in her nightie in middle of field surrounded by herd of cows," Alan chuckled.

"I were lucky it were only cows, you'd not get him near a bull," Aggie said nodding at Alan.

"Oh I'd have still done same thing me sweet," Alan said pursing his lips together and kissing the back of his wife's hand. "You and your Anty Eileen were very brave today though Gerald," Alan said as he smiled at Gerald.

Clive bundled into the house, after supper, ready for his evening's lodgings. Although Gerald felt closer to Clive now that they'd been through such a scary experience together, he was still not to be trusted. Gerald had seen what Clive had done to insects in the back garden and he didn't want that fate for Douglas but he didn't want to lose the bond that they'd formed between them either. Clive crossed the room and sat down next to Gerald.

"Where you been all day?" Clive asked.

"Oh just stayed here, played few games, nowt special. You?" Gerald replied, happy to be in pleasant conversation with Clive.

"Not much, shattered to be honest. Been an eventful day hasn't it?" he said yawning.

"Yeh sure has!" Gerald agreed.

Gerald glanced at the clock and wondered where Albert could be. He was sure that he would not be calling today now and so bid his goodnights and headed upstairs to bed. Gerald passed swiftly by Douglas' safe place, so as not to alert Clive to anything suspicious. He stripped off his clothes, donned his nightwear and slipped into the head end of the bed. A few moments later Clive slipped into the other end.

"Night Gerald," he whispered.

"Night Clive," Gerald replied and drifted peacefully into a deep sleep.

Day Ten

The Wrath of Sydney

Clive awoke with the delicious smell of a cooked breakfast wafting under his nose.

"Yum can you smell that Gerald!" he said, as he hurriedly descended the stairs, in search of the inviting aroma. Gerald was already awake, he'd hardly slept. The image of the faceless people still rushing through his mind and the insecurity of Clive being so close to his companion, had made him restless. He'd heard his Uncle Alan leave for work early, as grocers do. He'd listened intently, as his Aunty Aggie's bed frame had scraped across the floor the moment his uncle had left. Gerald knew that she had diligently checked on Douglas and realised to his relief that he must still be sleeping soundly, otherwise she would have alerted him. Singing merrily, Aunty Aggie had headed for the kitchen to set to work on her decoy. Concerned that Clive would discover Douglas, she had conjured up plans of her own to keep the impish boy from doing any harm. She'd created a feast of a breakfast to entice the greedy boy downstairs, using much of her weekly rations in the process.

Gerald had taken in the inviting odour too and although his stomach craved the texture and taste of the cooked breakfast, he knew it would be safe upstairs now for a while.

Taking the opportunity to look in on Douglas, he climbed quietly out of bed and peered at his grandpa.

"Grandpa," he whispered but the old man was still sound asleep. Satisfied that he was still in a deep slumber and unlikely to wake until midmorning, he crept slowly out of his shared room and on to the landing. Gerald leant over the wooden bannister and momentarily eavesdropped on the events in the kitchen; he knew that Clive would not leave the table until he'd had his fill. Content that Clive would not be coming back upstairs any time soon Gerald entered his auntie's room closing the door behind him.

Not sure what to expect he carefully lifted Douglas out of his secret hideaway hoping that the warmth would come through again as yesterday's coldness had frightened him. Gerald turned the ridged article over in his hands and examined the exterior of the cocoon. Its markings were striking, like the contours of a map. Without thinking, his mind filled with the words of his teacher pointing out the significance of all the pink bits on the world map. "The British Empire," Gerald recalled she had boomed proudly. Gerald ran his fingers over the bumpy exterior and traced the lines; the shape reminded him of something, a country perhaps but he'd never really taken much notice in geography.

"I'll ask Albert later what he thinks," he said thoughtfully. Gerald placed Douglas back in his safe haven and vacated the room.

It had been Gerald's intention to stand guard over his friend for most of the morning, even feigning illness if he had to. He'd planned to keep himself upstairs then make a miraculous recovery when Albert arrived, but as he listened intently to the mumbled sounds of Clive and Aunty Aggie enjoying their morning meal, he felt an overwhelming surge to join them. His stomach growled, as it always did when he was hungry and the thought of eggs and bacon only made it worse. Eventually his resistance waned, caving into the tantalising smell and he bounded down the stairs to feast on the banquet. He was expecting Kim to greet him, as she usually did, but uncharacteristically, she lay exhausted in her basket in front of the hearth.

"Morning sweetheart," Aunty Aggie said brightly. "Don't worry your sen about her," she said seeing his concern for the dog. "She's just tired out after yesterday's jaunt and she'll be fine later you'll see. Come and eat summat, before Clive eats it all!" Gerald stroked Kim gently and then eagerly pulled up a chair next to his gorging cousin and wasted no time in tucking into the special treat himself. The plan was going well, Clive was preoccupied with his food and the morning was ticking along nicely, ensuring Douglas' concealment for a while longer. When breakfast was over, Aggie encouraged the boys to help with the washing-up and secured their company further with welcoming mugs of sweet piping hot tea. She wasn't used to having guests and she was enjoying the morning's company greatly.

"AGGIE! AGGIE!" a high-pitched panicky voice yelled at the front door. "Hide our Clive, quick." Without a second thought, Aggie ushered the boys out of the kitchen and towards a stricken Florence.

"What's happened Florrie?" she asked.

"It's old man Johnson. He's after him! Someone's gone and told him they saw Clive on Friday crossing field, pulling summat." Aggie turned to look at Clive.

"Oh you dint!" she scolded. Clive grinned and Gerald blushed.

"He's livid, Aggs! Come over all aggressive with me. I were right glad Charlie were home otherwise I'd not have got him out of doorway," Florence said a little shaken. "Said that I'd seen him over near fields to bide us some time because he said he were coming to you next, so I got here as fast as I could!"

"You'd better hide Clive," Aggie said sternly. Clive didn't need telling twice and like a shot he ran towards the stairs in search of a safe place to hide. Gerald was horrified; he knew that if he let him go upstairs, he'd opt to hide in Aggie's room. Grandpa would have had no qualms in giving him away, he'd probably even take pleasure in it and Clive knew it.

"You can't hide up there Clive," Gerald said frantically as he blocked his path.

"Get out of my way you idiot!" Clive shouted as he swiftly pushed Gerald aside. "I'm not staying down here to face Johnson's wrath," Clive yelled. Gerald toppled sideways, his skinny physique no match for the bulkier frame of Clive.

Gerald pulled himself up and stared anxiously at the ceiling, waiting to hear which room Clive would chose to hide in.

"Oh no!" he sighed as he heard the metal bed frame scrape along the floor and the wooden floorboards creak.

"What's up Gerald?" Aunty Aggie asked quietly as she heard his sigh.

"He's under your bed!"

Aggie looked up at the ceiling and then glanced at her fraught sister and whispered, "Well there's nowt we can do for now. We'll just have to wait and hope that he doesn't see box." Gerald's head drooped in dismay. He knew Clive and doubted that he'd miss something which lay right under his nose.

"He's coming," Florence yelled.

"Gerald, run and fetch your uncle and tell him to hurry!" Aggie instructed as she hurried him out of the door.

Gerald was reluctant to leave the house for fear that Sydney would lash out at him, but he knew he needed to get help as Sydney Johnson was a big man and the two sisters were no match for his huge frame.

Aggie quickly latched the door behind her and turned to her sister. Taking Florence's hands in hers she stared deeply into her eyes.

"Listen sis, you and I both know Clive's probably as guilty as hell but Eileen will never forgive us if we don't defend him and I'd much sooner be an enemy of Sydney's than hers," Aggie said.

"He were so angry Aggie," she whimpered.

"We'll just have to stall him till Alan gets here," Aggie said reassuringly. Aggie had a persuasive manner, but she was not so sure that even her sweet-talking was going to dissuade Mr Johnson today.

Sydney Johnson had not always been so bad tempered; he was once a jovial character, who had lots of true friends, but when his first wife had died prematurely, it had changed him, making him bitter and withdrawn. Sydney and his wife had been inseparable, childhood sweethearts from the age of 14, they were devoted to one another and Mr Johnson had been devastated when she had died. As the years passed, his sadness prevailed and in his later years he turned to drink to drown his sorrows for the best friend he had lost.

When Lorna Davies arrived in the village, the locals were delighted when Sydney struck up a friendship with her, as she seemed to reignite a flame in him that had been lost for some time. Lorna won over almost everyone she met with her charming ways. On the face of it she couldn't do enough to help anyone in need. For the first time, in a very long time, Mr Johnson was beginning to be the man he once was and everyone was thrilled that, after a respectable two years courting, he chose to take Lorna to be his wife.

Almost immediately after the wedding, Lorna's true colours began to shine through. For a woman of such short stature, she was extremely domineering and took great delight in using Mr Johnson's true affection for her, to manipulate and belittle him at any given opportunity. She relished in making him the butt of her jokes and often made him look so foolish that you could see him physically squirm. His friends had tried to make him see sense, but Mr Johnson shunned their remarks as he was afraid of losing yet another love and feared being alone once again. Treated like a fool daily by his tiny wife, he lashed out with his frustration and anger on anyone else that dared to behave that way towards him.

Clive's antics last summer had made him angry, as it had upset his wife greatly when Clive had been caught stealing her gooseberries, but the grief that his wife had given him then was nothing compared to the humiliation that he now felt at being so easily tricked by such a young boy.

Sydney hated nothing more than being made to look a fool. He had tolerated his wife's treatment of him for years, as it was never normally constant. Sydney knew that this year's baking competition had been so important to Lorna that she'd drag out her disappointment for years, relishing telling anyone that would listen, that it was all his fault that the apples were stolen. The thought of Lorna using this unfortunate episode to get everyone to laugh at his weakness and stupidity was too much for him to bear and did nothing but fuel his anger.

BANG! BANG! BANG! Aggie's door shook under the thunderous knock. Aggie rose slowly and gingerly approached the door.

142

"Who is it?" she croaked.

"Where's the little villain?" came the reply.

"I don't know who you mean," Aggie replied in a silky voice.

"That damned nephew of Florence's, I know he's in there. He's gone and stolen all my Lorna's prizewinning apples!" raged Mr Johnson.

"Oh I am sure you're mistaken Sydney, Clive wouldn't do such a thing!" persuaded Aggie. Mr Johnson was not pleased, fury swelled in his chest, his fists clenched, his face turned red and with sheer anger he forced open the door.

"Get out me way Aggie," he shouted. "I'm coming to get the little brat." Mr Johnson thrust his size 12 boot over Aggie's threshold and used his huge mass to try and force his way into the house. Aggie and Florence barricaded the door in the hope that their joint weight would prevent him from getting in.

"This isn't achieving anything Sydney," Aggie counselled, but Sydney was determined and with a final thrust, he forced open the door, toppling the sisters to the ground. To the big man's horror, when he crashed into the house he fell within an inch of a snarling Kim.

"Grrrrrrrrr," she growled as Johnson steadily lifted himself off the floor. Kim did not take kindly to people hurting Aggie, she was extremely protective of her and Johnson knew it.

"Steady on now then Kim," he soothed as he backed slowly towards the open door.

"GGGRRRRRR," she growled again baring all of her teeth. Johnson stepped off the threshold, on to the terraced street, only to be greeted by an equally protective, Uncle Alan.

"I think it's about time you left now! Don't you Sydney?" Alan said with a firm hand grasping Sydney's right shoulder.

Confronted by two equally angry foes, the old man bowed away from the situation and left quicker than he had arrived.

"You two OK?" Alan asked as he helped the two women to their feet.

"Yeh we're fine," Aggie said dusting down her apron.

"Good job you came when you did though," Florence said relieved.

"Why's he so angry anyway?" Alan enquired.

The two sisters glanced at one another and then said simultaneously, "Clive."

"Clive? Why what's he been up to?" Alan asked, looping his arm around his wife. "Agatha I think you'd best tell me what's going on!" Aggie pursed her lips, shrugged her shoulders and set about telling him a little of what she knew.

Still hiding, Clive listened carefully for the commotion to die down so that he would know when it was safe to go back downstairs. Although he claimed not to be, he was scared of Mr Johnson and had no desire to be in his reach, but he knew that the wrath of his family could be much worse. He had to make them believe that he was innocent. Eileen had warned him, before they came down, to stay out of trouble or she'd have no choice than to tell his father and then his life wouldn't be worth living.

Clive knew that Aggie would have convinced Alan that it was all under control and that she would sort things out, so it was no surprise when he heard Alan leaving to go back to work. He knew he'd have to get Gerald on board. He was a good and frequent liar, but he was such a goody two shoes he'd have to do something to make him do it. Believing that the coast was clear he wriggled his way out, dislodging a loose floorboard from under the bed in the process. Swiftly, Clive ran round to the other side and lifted the plank to replace it, but was intrigued by the handcrafted box hidden below the loose timber. Clive reached underneath the floorboard and slid back the ventilated lid; he was dazzled by what he saw.

Mischief once again filled his eyes. He lifted the enormous cocoon out of its box and examined it carefully. He couldn't comprehend the magnitude of the chrysalis but he knew exactly what it was, Susan wasn't the only one with brains. The sheer size of its shell made Clive very excited and now he had his bargaining tool, as he had no doubt who it belonged to. He smirked as he began to understand why Gerald had fought so hard to keep him from going upstairs, his objection over him staying at his Aunty Aggie's house and his urgency to get round there so quick, all made perfect sense now. Clive was no fool.

"There must be something pretty special about you," he scoffed, "if he's going to all this trouble to keep it from me." Clive rolled the sleeping caterpillar in his hands and considered his next move.

He would need to play this cool if he was going to get what he wanted out of this scenario. Gerald was amongst friends in this house, he was sure Aggie would know all about it and as Gerald was rather chummy with Albert he was confident he was in cahoots with him too. Clive would have to leave the freakish object where it was for now and come and collect it later.

"He'll think I haven't seen it, if it's here when he comes to check," he thought out loud to himself. Clive congratulated himself on his master plan, replaced Douglas and left the room.

"Well lad, what do you have to say for your sen?" Aggie and Florence scorned in unison as Clive passed Gerald on the bottom step of the stairs. Clive was nonchalant in his response and tried hard to play down the old man's histrionics.

"Oh you know he's got it in for me, always has!" said Clive dismissively. "And anyway where would I put a tree full of apples?" The sisters didn't respond because they had no answer to his question but they knew he was guilty, he was just very crafty.

Gerald descended the stairs with more colour in his cheeks than he had on his ascending, his face veiled with relief. Clive grinned to himself, pleased that his plan was falling into place. The two aunties trailed off into the kitchen, leaving Clive and Gerald alone.

"What are we going do now Clive? What if Johnson finds them apples," said Gerald.

"Shh! He'll never find them. The hole's being filled on Friday, I've checked! You have to say it WASN'T ME! We made a pact Gerald!" Clive hissed. "You'll do as I say Gerald or you may end up regretting it!" Gerald knew his cousin could be a bit of a bully, but he was sure that his threat had not been a physical one. He wasn't sure what he meant but he knew that the lid on their secrets needed to be kept firmly shut.

Kim growled at Clive as he left the house, she had sensed Gerald's fear and raced to protect him. She had already had one of her loved ones attacked today; it wasn't going to happen twice on her watch. The rest of the day passed by with very few hitches, the threat of one angry man and his equally angry dog had been enough to keep Sydney from returning. Florence had returned home with the unenviable task of explaining things to Eileen, without incriminating Clive in any way and Aggie set about the rest of her chores.

The evening had come and gone and yet again Albert had not arrived to collect Douglas. Gerald was concerned for his friend but more anxious that he'd have to hide Douglas from Clive for one more night. He wasn't convinced that Clive hadn't seen Douglas when he was hiding under the bed and wondered what game he was playing by not saying anything. Aggie was of the same opinion but she could think of nowhere else to hide him, so he would have to stay where he was.

"We'll just have to be more vigilant and watch him like an hawk," she said, but Gerald knew he was in for yet another sleepless night.

Day Eleven
Kim to the Rescue

The morning came and Gerald rushed to check that
Douglas was still in his place. He'd tried hard to keep awake
but the restless night's sleep the evening before had caught
up with him and he'd fallen into a deep slumber. Albert
must surely come today he thought, it was stressful having
Clive and Douglas under the same roof. Gerald entered his
auntie's room and pushed back the bed frame in search of
his friend, but to his horror, Douglas was no longer there.

"Maybe me Anty Aggie's moved him," he said calmly
to himself, remembering the conversation that they'd had
the evening before. Gerald reached into the space but the
box was still in there. Surely if Aggie was going to move
him, she'd have moved the lot. "Clive!" he said angrily and
started to panic. He hadn't been in his bed when Gerald had
awoken and neither had his grandpa. Feeling that Douglas
was in danger, Gerald ran straight back into his bedroom,
put on the first clothes that he could find and raced down
the stairs and into the kitchen. "AGGIE! ANTY AGGIE!"
Gerald yelled.

"Whatever's the matter Gerald?" she asked him calmly.

His aunty was standing over the top of his very grumpy
grandpa, who was having his daily shave and monthly trim.
Grandpa was not a good customer and disliked having

his face scraped; he demanded complete silence whilst it was being done, he had been a prisoner in the First World War and blamed that for his fear of sharp blades. Gerald knew how mean Grandpa could be when he was afraid, many a time he'd caught the rough end of his walking stick just for coughing while the delicate procedure was being performed; but Gerald wasn't going to be silenced today.

He slid swiftly by his grandpa and sidled up to his aunty. "Douglas isn't in his box!" he whispered quietly in her ear. Aggie in full flow, jolted with horror when her nephew spoke, her hand lost precision and the knife quickly nicked Grandpa's cheek.

"Ow you stupid woman, are you trying to kill me!" Grandpa cried out and hurriedly stood up from the table. Wrapping his towel tightly around his injury, he left the room muttering to himself, "It's like flaming Sweeney Todd's in here!"

"Have you moved him?" Gerald pleaded hopefully, but Aggie had not. "Where's Clive?" he asked through gritted teeth.

"I don't know love. He went out straight after breakfast."

"I'm going to me Mam's, to see if he's there, I'll be back in a bit," said Gerald. Grandpa launched a swipe with his cane but Gerald dodged him, ran out the door and around the corner to his house.

As he approached his home, he saw the familiar stance of PC Joyce standing outside his front door. From the inside of the house he could just glimpse his Aunty Eileen standing protectively in the doorway. Gerald wasn't sure he was in the mood to be interrogated today, as he had a crime of his own to solve.

"Morning Gerald," PC Joyce spoke in his usual official voice. "I was just asking your aunty here about these missing apples. We've had a witness come forward and say they saw some kids up near the orchard last Friday pulling a trolley, know anything about it son?" asked PC Joyce.

Gerald wanted to scream out that it was all Clive's idea and it was him that he wanted. He wanted to take PC Joyce to the buried apples there and then and let Clive hang out to dry; he was so angry that he'd taken Douglas. Gerald knew that he couldn't divulge anything because Clive had been clever and made them all his accomplices. More than that, he feared what Clive would do to Douglas if he did tell and he couldn't risk that!

"No sir, I were at Albert's on Friday, sorry," Gerald replied convincingly. Happy that he had satisfied PC Joyce, Gerald turned to his aunty. "Is Clive here Anty Eileen?" Gerald asked anxiously.

"Yes I think so Gerald, have a look around the back, I think he's out in the garden with Alfie," replied Eileen suspiciously.

"Thanks Anty Eileen," Gerald shouted back as he raced down the side alley and into the garden, leaving her to grill her old fiancé for the identity of the witness. Tom Joyce was well aware of her tactics, but was so pleased to have her slightest attention and the opportunity to talk to Eileen that he let her exploit his adoration to her full advantage.

When Gerald reached the back garden, there was no sign of either Clive or Alfie and so he hurriedly raced back inside.

"ANTY EILEEN, they're not in garden!" exclaimed Gerald.

"Hello stranger, I dint see you come in! Who's not in garden?" his mother replied.

"CLIVE!" he yelped beginning to panic.

"Praps he's gone to your Anty Aggie's house," she offered in reply.

"Where's Susan Mam?" Gerald asked.

"She's upstairs I think. Whatever's the matter Gerald?" his mother asked. Gerald didn't answer. Relieved to see Susan at the top of the stairs, he beckoned his favourite cousin down. He needed help and Susan was the only one he could trust.

Susan came when she was bid. "What's wrong Gerald?" Susan enquired leaning in close so that the mothers couldn't hear him reply.

"It's Clive, I think he's got Douglas!" he whispered. "I just know he has Susan! He made out he dint see nothing tuther day, but I've just got a feeling he's up to no good," Gerald said desperately. The two friends ran quickly along the street to Aggie's house in search of their siblings.

"Any joy?" Aggie asked as Gerald opened the kitchen door.

"No, no sign of them! Don't suppose they came back here?" Gerald replied in a small voice. Aggie hadn't heard anyone come in, she'd been busy clearing away after his grandpa's haircut and Kim hadn't made a sound, she'd been very quiet all morning.

Gerald tiptoed slowly into the back room, so as not to disturb his dozing grandpa and bent down to stroke Kim.

"Is she ill?" Gerald asked concerned.

"I don't think so. She were fine last night, a little tired after her bullfight but were right as rain later on," Aggie replied. The three comrades sat around the meek dog and pondered about where Douglas could have gone and where the two boys could be. Gerald knew why Clive had taken him, but he didn't want to jeopardise the hostage's release by telling his Aunty Aggie about the missing apples.

Aggie stood up and wandered into the kitchen to make tea, while the two cousins remained with Kim. Susan stretched out her hand and tapped Gerald gently on his arm.

"Can you smell that Gerald?" Susan said pointing to Kim's mouth. Gerald looked curiously at Susan and bowed down towards Kim. He drew level with her mouth and inhaled deeply, then withdrew quickly as he took in the strong musty aroma.

"Wow, that's really strong. What is it?" he said.

"It's smells like she's been drinking whiskey!" Susan replied.

"What's up with you two?" Aggie asked, as she walked back into the room, carrying three mugs of piping hot tea. The children said nothing; they were staring at each other in disbelief. Kim had been doped and they knew exactly who had done it. Gerald had been seething before, but Clive had surpassed himself now.

"I think Kim's drunk Aggie!" Susan exclaimed.

"What? Don't be daft!" Aggie said lowering the tea on to the coffee table. She cupped her hands either side of her precious dog's head and drew her in close to sniff her breath taking in the familiar mouldy smell. She knew the scent well; Grandpa reeked of it daily and had fermented her house with its odour since his arrival.

Aggie breathed a deep annoyed sigh, rose slowly from the side of her intoxicated dog and walked determinedly towards the kitchen. After a few moments she returned with two large bowls of water, which she placed carefully on the floor. Dropping to her knees, Aggie cradled Kim's limp head in her left hand and pulled the first bowl of water under her chin with her right. Kim didn't stir at first, but with some gentle persuasion she started to lap up the refreshing liquid until the bowl was drained.

"She needs to drink as much as possible to sober her up, if she's sick it'll burn her throat out," Aggie instructed with tears welling in her eyes.

The children took over the role of nursemaid while Aggie fetched and carried endless vessels of cold water. After an hour Kim started to recover, displaying a few characteristics of her usual boisterous character.

Aggie wiped her eyes with the edge of her apron and looked both of them straight in the eye and said firmly, "We need to find Clive!" The children could see that she was relieved that her precious dog was more like her old self but behind her teary eyes, she was seething that Clive had fed her dog alcohol.

Susan and Gerald sat for a while and contemplated where Clive and Alfie could have gone but they had no need to search very far, as right above them hidden under the bed were the culprits themselves. The two boys had been panic-stricken when they heard the cousins come home and had taken refuge under Aggie's bed. They lay perfectly still, eavesdropping and awaiting their opportunity to escape with Douglas.

After his lucky escape from Sydney, Clive had set his mind on stealing the one thing that he was certain would guarantee Gerald's silence. The true master plan had started the previous day, when he'd left the house. He knew that Kim didn't like him and so in order to prevent her from stopping him getting out of the house with the cocoon he had come up with a plan to stop her. After collecting Alfie and stealing Grandpa's hidden stash of whiskey from his allotment, Clive had soaked Kim's evening meal in the booze and hidden it away.

When Clive had returned to his auntie's house that evening, he'd insisted that he do chores to make up for the trouble he had caused with Sydney. Aggie had been so impressed with his keenness to please she had obliged and let him help out all he could. Usually Kim's evening meal was dished up by Aggie, just before she served the family meal, but on this night Clive had quickly stepped in and supplied Kim with her meal and the crime had gone undetected.

All had been going to plan. Clive had risen early, checked that Gerald was sound asleep and waited patiently for his Aggie to go downstairs before making his move. Once he was sure that she had gone into the kitchen he had taken the cocoon from its safe haven. Knowing that he had very little time before Gerald woke up he chose to just move the cocoon to another location. Clive had noticed the day before that some of the other planks under Aggie's bed were also loose and so he had simply lifted another plank and put the cocoon inside, leaving the wooden box with the lid where it was. Clive had slipped down the stairs undetected to check that Kim was still docile and seeing that the big dog was still in a deep slumber, he had grinned menacingly believing it was safe to continue with his plan.

Clive, not wanting to arouse suspicion, had breakfast with Aggie, as he would ordinarily do and then went straight out in search of Alfie. Alfie had only agreed to help Clive, when he had been convinced that Kim wasn't going to wake up. Clive was banking on Gerald coming out of the house, in search of him, so that he could get back in and steal Gerald's prize possession. The duo had waited for Gerald to leave the house for a while and had taken refuge in an open but empty house across the street. Aggie had told Clive earlier that morning that she would be cutting his grandpa's hair, so he was sure he'd be able to sneak in again without detection.

Through the muffled sounds, the boys had heard the discovery of Clive's mischief and Alfie had started to panic.

Alfie was terrified of Kim and his encounters with the bullocks on Sunday had made his nerves even worse. Clive knew they couldn't wait any longer or Alfie would lose his bottle altogether. The downstairs inhabitants had appeared to have moved into the front room, so Clive seized his chance and slid from underneath the bed, holding Douglas firmly in his grasp.

"Come on Alfie, you're not scared are you!" he mocked. Alfie didn't want to go, but knew he'd be in for more teasing if he didn't, so he crawled from under the bed to join his cousin.

Checking that the landing was clear and that the back room was empty of voices, Clive made his descent down the creaky stairs.

He had almost made it to the bottom step when Alfie tapped him on the shoulder and asked in a shaky voice, "What's that noise?" Clive craned to listen; coming from the front room to the back he could hear a gentle tip tapping, a familiar shuffling and a breathy panting. "It's Kim, isn't it?" Alfie shuddered with fear. Clive turned immediately to Alfie and lifted his finger to his lips in annoyance.

"Shush you idiot," he said. They listened and waited for the patroller to return to her usual spot beside the fire in the front room, but the movement had stopped.

The boys listened intently as they heard Kim slump to the floor at the foot of the stairs and commence her normal grooming routine.

"Oh for goodness' sake she's licking herself now!" Clive said in exasperation.

"We can't stay here Clive!" said a tearful Alfie.

"What do you suggest we do then genius?" Clive said angrily.

"Let's go back upstairs and put it back, Clive!" he said pleadingly. Clive looked at his terrified cousin and agreed that it was the only solution. They wouldn't be able to sneak out the back door with Kim in the way and he definitely didn't want to be discovered with this stolen cargo in tow.

The twosome began to slowly step backwards up the creaky stairs but their ascent did not go unnoticed. Kim's astute ears heard the squeak and they instinctively pricked up to attention. She immediately stopped her preening and shuffled curiously to where the noise was coming from. Alfie screamed and ran to hide upstairs, as Kim's sniffing nose peeped around the corner. Her eyes locked on the two scoundrels.

"Grrrrrr," she growled through her rolled back lips, revealing small yellow and very sharp teeth.

Clive wasn't afraid of the dog and so he kicked out at her in an attempt to make her move out of the way.

"Get back you stupid dog!" he hissed. Kim was not fond of Clive and his aggressive actions just fuelled her irritation. She yapped and snapped aggressively at him; her hackles were up and she'd set her eyes on him. Clive launched another attack on Kim but she was too quick for him, she went for his laces and in one momentous tug she propelled him down the stairs. Clive landed ungainly in a heap at the bottom and was swiftly incarcerated by Kim's slobbering mouth firmly around his throat.

"Let him be, Kim," Aggie commanded in a controlled voice. Kim was reluctant to withdraw her grasp on her prisoner and growled as she glared into Clive's terrified eyes. "Let go Kim!" Aggie commanded again and with a grumble she released her victim from her grip. Aggie took Kim by the collar, restrained her by the lead in the back kitchen and then returned to the bottom of the stairs. She took Clive's face in her hands and examined his neck. The skin was not broken and apart from being a little shocked after his traumatic experience, he was OK. Aggie removed the chrysalis from Clive's grip, which he relinquished guiltily, and handed it gently back to Gerald.

Aggie turned back to Clive, grabbed him angrily by the scruff of his neck and said in a trembling voice, "There's a lot I could say to you right now lad and I did warn this would happen last time you misbehaved in me house but it sempt like you've been taught a big lesson today already and one you're unlikely to forget, so I'm going to say nowt more about it." Clive looked up at Aggie's stern face and he knew that she was seething with anger. He rubbed his throat as she relinquished her grip and nodded his head. His eyes filled with tears and for the first time in his life he realised that he really had gone too far.

"I'm sorry," he sobbed as he hugged Aggie tightly. "I'm really sorry."

Gerald looked down at Douglas, safe in his hands and breathed a sigh of relief. He looked at his cousin wrapped in his Aunty Aggie's forgiving embrace and hoped that in time he would too feel more compassion for his cousin. Still teeming with anger, Gerald slid by Clive and headed upstairs to put Douglas back in his retreat. As he climbed the stairs, he saw Alfie clinging to the bannister. He wanted to be angry with Alfie too, but he could see how frightened he was and knew he was as much a victim of Clive's cruel schemes as he had been. Gerald plonked himself on the stair next to his sibling and furled his free arm around his shaking shoulders.

"It's OK Alfie. Anty Aggie's tied her up!" Gerald said comfortingly.

Alfie lifted his head from between his knees, wiped his eyes and pointed at the strange object held tightly in Gerald's grasp.

"What is it anyway?" Alfie asked. Gerald held the brown ridged shell up for them both to see and smiled.

"He don't look much does he? Not while he's sleeping, but soon he'll be awake and then I hope I'll know what he really is," Gerald said hopefully. As the words left his lips, he felt the warmth from the cocoon soar through its outer shell. Gerald didn't need any images or words to tell him what to do next, he had someone he loved in need of support and the reassuring warmth emanating from Douglas was enough to tell him he was doing OK on his own.

Day Twelve
Buried

Aggie arrived early on the Friday morning at the Hughes household, dressed in her funeral blacks. She had returned Clive to Florence's house on the Thursday afternoon and he'd stayed there with Alfie for the night. The trauma had been too great for him to stay at Aggie's house any longer. Florence had said that she was happy to have him home as Billy and Charlie were returning to official duty that evening, and so was grateful that Alfie wouldn't have to be on his own.

For a quiet life, Aggie had chosen to keep silent about the alcohol in Kim's system and Clive's misguided actions. Eileen had just been told that Clive had a run-in with the dog and that now he too was afraid, hence his desire to return to the homestead. Florence, who knew there'd be more to the scenario, got almost the full story and agreed that it was best for everyone if Eileen was kept in the dark. Gerald, who had no desire to be within 3 ft. of his cousin, had pleaded to stay at his auntie's house and he'd been allowed to stay as he was not afraid of the dog.

"You should have that dog put down Agatha, she's a menace, first the bullocks and now my little Clive!" Eileen barked, as Aggie walked into Florence's front room. Aggie didn't retaliate; it was a battle that she'd never win while Eileen was ignorant of the entire story.

"I'll keep tight lead on her Eileen from now on, but no real harm done by DOG though eh! So no need to take it any further now is there?"

Eileen agreed, but the sarcasm, which Aggie had laid on so thickly, was wasted on her. She was a smart lady, who had no qualms about what her son was really like; she was fully aware that he could be devious, but there was a difference between her knowing it and everyone else. Eileen had a reputation to uphold and she certainly wasn't going to admit to any failing of her own.

Florence, however, noted her sister's tone, as she too knew what trouble Clive could cause. She'd had her suspicions over the years that he'd been responsible for more than her sister-in-law cared to admit. She'd watched Eileen smooth things over wherever she could and how wagging tongues got quickly silenced. Florence was convinced that Clive was the ringleader behind the missing apples and wondered how Eileen would silence Lesley Osbourne since she had discovered, from PC Joyce, it had been her who'd been spreading the rumours.

Eileen was a devoted mother and went to great pains to make sure all her children received equal attention. When Clive had come downstairs, she had ushered him to get his cooked breakfast and fussed over her middle child until she was happy that her duty was done and then set her attentions on Josie.

"Come on then Josie," she beamed, "let's get cooking." Tomorrow was the village fete and Josie had insisted that they bake a pie for the competition. Eileen pondered whether Mrs Johnson would enter this year, now that she had no apples left on her famous tree to bake with. "I think we could win this year sweetheart," she chirruped to Josie.

Josie hauled the bag of scrumped cooking apples on to the table and looked at her mum. "Me too Mummy, I think we've got very lucky apples!"

Florence left Eileen and Josie to bake and made her way with Aggie towards the graveyard. The local butcher had died a few days before and today was his funeral. All the local shops had closed out of respect for this pillar of the community. He was a well-liked man and all who knew him would be expected to attend. Josie was too young to go to the funeral, so the baking served as a good distraction for the determined little girl, but the cousins were told that they should be seen to be showing their respects and if they didn't want to go too close to the grave, they could watch from the sides.

The two sisters strode ahead and were pleased, but surprised that all four of the cousins were brave enough to join them, despite yesterday's ordeal. The butcher lived across the street from the cemetery and so the service was to be held around the graveside and not in church which was the usual custom. The mourners gathered in their droves to watch the pall-bearers carry the butcher's coffin the short distance from his home to his resting place. The midmorning heat penetrated through their dark attire and their faces grimaced under the butcher's heavy weight.

The grave had been dug well in advance, as they always were, and the earth from inside the tomb was piled high at the side. A crowd congregated around the deep hole and stared sadly into the dark pit. Florence glanced at the familiar faces circling the grave, she acknowledged the ones that she only recognised by sight and searched amongst the crowd for the ones she knew well. Mrs Osbourne was missing, which was unusual, as she loved any sort of gathering. She noticed that Albert was nowhere to be seen either and she was surprised and disappointed at the same time. He'd been away for a while now and his recent absence and secrecy was giving her cause for concern.

As the coffin approached the graveside, Susan ran to Florence's side and broke her trance. She interlocked her fingers with her auntie's and held her hand tightly.

"You OK?" Florence asked as she reciprocated her niece's squeeze.

"I'm a little scared actually Aunty Florrie, I have never been to a funeral before," she replied.

"It'll be OK ducky, it's not so bad when it's not someone you love," comforted Florence.

Clive was scouring the crowd too and when he spotted the object of his desire, he broke free from the group. Florence, who was wary of Clive, was watching him closely; his hasty movement had attracted her attention. Peering around the hordes of people, Florence looked bemused as she watched Clive sidle up to Mrs Johnson, who was standing centre stage at the end of the grave.

"Susan why would your brother want to stand next to someone he claims to hate so much?" Florence turned to her niece for her reply. Susan winced showing obvious signs of discomfort at being asked that question. "What's he up to Susan?" Florence coaxed.

Susan scuffed the ground with her black patent shoe in annoyance. "I can't tell you Aunty Florrie, I promised!"

"Susan if he's in some sort of trouble I need to know now!" Susan gravely lifted her head and stared deep into her auntie's blue eyes.

"He's told me this is the end of it, no more nonsense, he's achieved what he set out to achieve and that's that! Please don't ask me anymore questions Aunty Florrie, a promise is a promise and I don't want to break it," explained

Susan. Florence looked into Susan's beautiful big, honest blue eyes and smiled.

"OK sweetheart as long as he has everything covered, I'll not say another word."

"Thanks Aunty Florrie," Susan grinned, relieved that it was not she who would break the pact.

Lorna Johnson had looked none too pleased when Clive had flanked her but as the occasion had warranted it, she put aside her obvious hatred for Clive and had turned to him and gave him a wistful smile.

Unnerved by the closeness of her adversary, Lorna Johnson could hold her silence no longer and spoke. "Sad isn't it, that he won't be judging the pie competition this year?" When there came no response from Clive, Lorna turned to look at him. "Young man, did you hear me?" Clive said nothing he just waited, watching intently as the coffin approached the grave he himself had inhabited only a few days before.

Mrs Johnson fidgeted uncomfortably as she observed Clive staring like a madman at the pall-bearers, as they placed the massive coffin on to the straps which would lower the butcher into his dark tomb. Clive's heart was beating fast now, as he silently egged the men on as they shuffled along the green matting lying either side of the gaping hole. He gulped hard as he watched them lower the butcher to his final resting place, remembering how terrified he had felt as he vengefully spread the apples.

Out of respect for the butcher, Clive waited until the prayers were finished and the grave was almost full before he spoke. He didn't need to say much but what he did say needed to be enough to let Lorna Johnson know what was in the grave alongside the butcher. Taking a deep breath he turned very slowly towards Mrs Johnson, bent down so that his hands rested on his thighs and patted her gently on her shoulder. Mrs Johnson turned begrudgingly towards Clive, still smarting that he had not responded to her earlier chit-chat.

Lorna stared indignantly at Clive with her mean piggy eyes.

"What?" she scorned her role as mourner now over.

Clive moved his face as close as he could to the old woman's and whispered in reply to her previous comment, "Yes it is sad Mrs Johnson, but a compliment don't you think... that he chose to take your prizewinning apples with him eh?"

"What?" she hissed in disbelief. "What do you mean?" she squealed as she glared back and forth from Clive to the grave.

The corners of Clive's mouth began to curl as he basked in the vile little woman's misery.

"Are you saying my apples are in that grave!" pointed Mrs Johnson. Clive pushed his hands deep into his short's pocket pulled out an apple and gave it to Mrs Johnson.

"Yes, all accept this one, if it's any good to you? Not enough to make a pie with I know, but diced up with a bit of sugar it would make a tasty snack." Lorna stared down at the solitary fruit which Clive had nestled into the palm of her hand and the disbelief she had felt, quickly turned to anger.

"You stupid, foolish boy, have you any idea what you've done!" she said as she spun her head round in search of her husband. "Sydney! Sydney!" she yelled at the top of her voice.

"Mrs Johnson! Mrs Johnson!" Clive cooed as he patted her yet again on her shoulder.

"What?" she replied.

"This is for you!" Clive pulled from his other pocket an envelope and handed it to her.

"What's that?" she scolded, gesturing towards the letter.

Clive shrugged his shoulders and said, "It's from my mother; she says it's my insurance." Mrs Johnson frowned at Clive, snatched the envelope from his grip, and then tore it open and unfolded the letter enclosed within.

Nonchalantly Mrs Johnson's eyes trickled over Eileen's words as she took in the letter's contents. As she read, the little colour that she had, drained from her face and her mean blue eyes glazed over with sadness and began to fill with tears. Clive watched as the old lady visibly squirmed with fear at the realisation that someone had the key to her deepest, darkest secrets. He didn't know what his mother had written on the page, now clasped tightly in his foe's hand, but from her reaction he knew that her silence was guaranteed.

"What's wrong love? Is this lad bothering you?" Mr Johnson said scowling at Clive as he reached his wife's side. Quickly Mrs Johnson hid the letter in her dress pocket, so that no one could see. She smiled thinly up towards her doting husband, wiped away the tears building in her eyes and shook her head gently.

Turning to look at Clive, she swallowed deeply and said, "You tell your mother... that... that some things are best left buried!" With that last statement, Mrs Johnson turned on her heel, stiffly linked arms with her husband and walked away from the hopes of winning the prize or ever reprimanding the culprit for stealing her apples.

Clive watched as his aggressor walked away with his tiny wife and he wondered if Mrs Johnson would scorn her husband for losing her the chance to win the large cash prize at the national event, as Clive had intended her to, or whether she would lay the entire business to rest. Clive regarded the odd-looking couple as they walked arm in arm in the distance, he thought about how awful Mrs Johnson could be towards her husband and concluded that she was bound to make her husband's life difficult for a while. He suspected though that her bitterness would not last forever, as the apples on the Johnson's big tree were bound be back again next year and with Mrs Johnson's baking skills and track record she would no doubt go on to win first prize again someday. Clive was sure though that the anger that she had felt this year would be lost completely should she do so, but for now he was satisfied that he had at least created a little misery in their lives, just as Mr Johnson had, in his last summer.

Clive knew he'd been a really naughty child and that he'd really gone too far, but he felt no remorse for what he'd done to the Johnson couple, he felt justified in his actions. He knew he truly deserved to be punished and that as usual he had his mum to thank for having such an ace up her sleeve to protect him. Without the ammunition his mother had tightly sealed in Mrs Johnson's letter he would have been in trouble with the law for sure.

He had not only been humiliated, when old man Johnson had hooked him on to the scarecrow last summer, he had been afraid. Sydney Johnson was a bully and he was tired of being bullied by men old enough to know better. He felt he needed to do something drastic, to show that he could stand up to his attackers and be strong enough to ensure that they would never hurt him again. Thanks to his mother, this was now guaranteed. He smiled to himself as he thought about how lucky he was to have a mother like her.

After such a dramatic episode with the dog the day before, Clive had been distraught and had begun to open up to his mum about all sorts of things. He was so afraid that he would get caught, he had done everything he could to keep everyone quiet and since he had been stopped so abruptly in his tracks, he had no choice other than to come clean with his mum. She had listened with tears in her eyes, knowing that she had not defended him enough against old man Johnson the previous summer and hadn't protected him enough either, inside his own home.

Eileen was not an outwardly aggressive person; she never used physical violence in her battles or demeaned herself by brawling in the street. She was an intelligent lady who used her wits to win her fights and did so with the information she was privy to. She had given him the ammunition to ensure that his misdemeanours would not come back to haunt him and had promised that his father would never hurt him again. He wasn't sure how she was going to accomplish this, as she was no match for the powerful Mr Challender, but he knew that whatever his mum set out to do, she always managed to achieve it. She was not one to renege on a promise, so he took comfort in that knowledge. Clive hoped that the bitterness that he felt inside would dissipate completely once his mother had tackled the problems within his own home, but it was going to take a great deal of courage, if she was to take the steps necessary to protect Clive from his aggressive father.

Clive made his way back to his family, who'd been watching his conversation with the old lady with interest.

"What were that all about Clive?" Aggie asked.

"You OK lad?" Florence echoed in concern.

Clive smiled faintly at the two sisters. "I have done some terrible things, which I am sure you know!" he said remorsefully. Florence and Aggie nodded in unison. "I am truly sorry for the things that have affected the people I love," he said glancing at Gerald. "But that was the last of them I promise. The fruits of evil are dead and buried,"

Clive said with a nod towards the grave.

"Oh Clive you dint?" Florence and Aggie said together in shocked voices realising what he had done.

"Won't he come after you?" Gerald piped up.

"No, she won't let that happen, or her reputation would be in tatters," Clive replied.

"What do you mean Clive?" Florence asked naïvely, but Aggie just shook her head.

"He means Eileen's put stop to it, of course," she said knowingly.

Clive grinned. "Yeh, you could say Mummy saved me."

Despite having been at a funeral, the family returned to the Hughes household in high spirits. Their good tempers rose further still as they opened the front door and inhaled the delicious aroma of freshly baked apple pie. The children bundled into the back kitchen, keen to see if there was enough pie to eat now, as well as to enter one for the fete and they weren't disappointed.

Josie jumped for joy when she saw them. "We're going to win," she whooped as she launched herself into her brother's arms.

"I believe that this young lady may well have a chance this year," said Albert as he leaned nonchalantly back in his chair, his mouth filled with pastry.

"Albert!" Gerald shouted as he ran into Albert's arms.

"Steady there Gerald, you'll jolly well have me over," Albert laughed as he steadied his chair.

"Where you been Albert? I've been right worried about you," asked Gerald.

"Oh there was no need for concern. I've simply been delayed in London for a while. I'm sorry I couldn't keep to our arrangement Gerald but I am sure you'll be delighted with the package that I have arriving tomorrow," Albert replied with a kindly wink. Gerald was intrigued to know what was in the package but he was not the only one with questions.

"Were surprised when you wasn't at butcher's funeral Albert," Florrie chirruped.

"Oh I couldn't face it Florrie. I have only just recovered from the last one I went to!" he replied. Florrie was unsure what he meant, she didn't know of any other funerals that had occurred locally in the last few months, so just assumed that it was an old war pal in London maybe. She didn't wish to pry so she let it pass.

"Eileen's just mashed Florrie, do you want a cuppa?" Aggie asked already nursing it in her fingers.

"Ooh that'd be lovely sis ta," Florence said as she gratefully accepted the fresh brew and perched herself on a seat next to Albert. Gerald was already in deep conversation with him, so she knew that there was little chance that Albert's attentions could be diverted to her. She watched them together sharing secrets, and although it warmed her heart to see two people she cared so deeply for happy in each other's company, she couldn't contain the pang of guilt and jealously that ran through her. Since Albert had rekindled his friendship with the family, she had come to realise how much she had missed him being in their lives and how happy she was to have him around again.

"Slice of apple pie Aunty Florrie?" Josie chirped breaking Florence's chain of thought.

"Ooh yes please sweetheart," Florence said as she took the plate offered by the proud little girl.

"Mum's put a blob of whipped cream on it too, but I think it tastes better without it," said Josie, a little annoyed at her mum's interference. Josie watched intently as Florence sunk her fork into the lightly browned crisp pastry. Florrie couldn't help but smile as she noticed Josie mirroring her mouth opening as she scooped up a decent portion without cream and raised the fork to her mouth.

"Mmm Josie this is amazing!" Florence chimed as she observed her small niece anxiously waiting her comments. "I think you just might win this year sweetie, especially now Mrs Johnson's not entering," Florence said smiling at Clive.

"Do you really think so Aunty Florrie?" Josie beamed. "It would be nice to have that trophy for a year."

"And don't forget the winner gets automatic entry into national baking competition this year," Aggie added.

"The £100 cash prize wouldn't go amiss either!" Eileen boomed out.

"Right, about time I were getting home," Aggie sighed, as she pushed back her chair and stood up from the table. "Alan will be back soon and wanting his egg and chips and Lord knows what Grandpa's been up to while I've been here all this time chatting and eating pie!" Florence agreed that it would be sensible to let Gerald continue to stay at his Aunty Aggie's until the cousins went home; it seemed silly to come home when there was more room at his auntie's house. Albert offered to walk the twosome home and after they had all said their goodbyes they headed for Aggie's place.

"Don't forget to tell Alan what a great pie those cookers he gave Josie have made," Eileen chuckled. Gerald wondered if Eileen knew the apples were from Lorna Johnson's tree, but knowing his Aunty Eileen, it would forever be a mystery.

Gerald chatted to Albert, as they walked slowly back to Aggie's house. He tried to fill him in with what had happened during the days that he'd been away, but there wasn't enough time to give him every detail that he'd missed in the last three days. When they reached Aggie's house his Uncle Alan was still not home and his grandpa was on his second nap of the morning, so the threesome made their way up the middle stairs in search of Douglas.

Albert held Douglas in his hands and examined his outer shell; he hadn't seen him in his chrysalis state.

Carefully he ran his fingers down the contours of his cocoon and without thinking Albert murmured to himself, "France!"

Gerald knelt down next to his friend and asked, "France?"

"Yes," Albert nodded. "The design on the outside of the shell, it resembles France."

Gerald laughed. "That's what it reminded me of; I knew you'd know Albert." Albert acknowledged his young friend's adoration with a wink and placed the precious object back into Gerald's hands.

Affectionately Albert touched the top of the young boy's head and said, "I have to go now Gerald but I'll see you tomorrow at the fete OK." Disappointed that he was leaving so soon, Gerald's face couldn't hide his feelings. "I'm sorry I haven't been here lately, Gerald, Albert said guiltily.

"Aren't you taking Douglas with you?" Gerald asked surprised.

"No Gerald, I think that it would be for the best if Douglas remained here with you, from now on." Aggie rose to say her farewells too. He kissed her gently on her cheek and they left the room, leaving Gerald deep in thought.

Unhappily, Gerald pushed himself back against the bed frame and drew his knees up to his chest. He looked down at the special gift in his palms and studied the strange object in front of him. Gerald thought about the magical fury creature encased inside and all the images that he'd shown him.

"What are you trying to tell me?" he said shaking it gently as if demanding an answer. Inquisitively he traced the lines on the outside of the shell, as Albert had, in the hope that his navigating around their contours would give him a clue. "France," he said thoughtfully.

Gerald's mind began to wander, as he strained to recall any details he may have retained from his geography lessons about France. He wished he'd paid more attention now to Mrs Reagan in class as she drummed in, fact after fact on her huge world map. Wracking his brains for anything to do with the country, he recalled the class's travels with Eckhart the Bear. Mrs Reagan had lovingly knitted her a special jumper for every trip to help them to remember the flags.

The red, white and blue striped jumper, proudly worn by Mrs Reagan's old teddy bear, appeared clearly in his mind. Within seconds, Gerald had made the French connection between the colours on the flag and Douglas' coloured fur, but he didn't understand why it was important. Frustrated and exhausted, Gerald bent his head down so that it lay on top of Douglas' shell, in the hope that he'd give him another clue, but nothing came. He was tired of these snippets of information being spoon-fed to him. He felt like an eavesdropper on Douglas' thoughts and feelings. Gerald guessed that the images that he had been privy to, must have been important memories, but why Douglas had shared them with him he didn't know.

Exasperated, Gerald rubbed his hands roughly through his hair and tried to piece together all the magic he'd been touched by so far. He understood with help of Mrs Reagan that it had something to do with France and he had started to make a link that someone had been hurt badly.

"But what's Anty Aggie's dead baby got to do with it?" he said, as he rolled Douglas around in his fingers.

Gerald lifted Douglas' stone-like shape above his head and examined him closely. Perhaps Douglas was a vessel to aid the hurting and that is why Aggie had been touched so because she needed healing. He'd heard of people with this gift, his mum had shooed them away when they came to the door selling raggedy bits of tat and lavender tied up with an odd bit of string. Gerald smiled at the memory of his mum and him hiding behind the curtains, when they saw the gypsies combing the streets for customers. He wondered how Douglas could help her, if he indeed could heal pain. She had been so sad for years since his dad had not returned from the war and at that moment Gerald realised that it was time that he shared his secret with his mum. Douglas would only be in his cocoon for two more days and he did not know what would happen when he was free to fly away, he knew that if Douglas was the tonic that his mum needed he had to show her soon.

He listened as he heard Albert leave the house and wondered if he knew more than he was letting on and questioned whether Douglas had shared intimate moments with him too. He hadn't seemed at all surprised when he'd told him about the images that he'd seen and his mouth had curled when Gerald had mentioned a familiar voice. He hoped that Albert did know what was happening and that one day he'd explain it to him. Carefully he wrapped Douglas in a pillowcase from Aggie's laundry basket and stowed Douglas away in his faithful knapsack. He'd show his mum tomorrow after the fete. He hoped that he was right and that Douglas did have magic powers, he also questioned whether he'd have the power to bring his dad home safely and then his mum would be truly happy.

Day Thirteen
The Second Saturday

Excitement radiated throughout the Hughes household as the morning of the village fete had finally arrived. Josie, who had received nothing but compliments on her apple pie yesterday, was coiled like a spring. She had been washed and dressed since early morning and had busied herself making her pie look the prettiest it could be, sprinkling it with caster sugar and pinching one of Susan's ribbons to make a huge bow, giving it that extra bit of glamour.

The Hughes family were a competitive bunch and had, as every year, maximised their chances of winning more prizes than any other family, by entering everything they possibly could. Second Saturday, as they had coined it, was a fantastic event and there was something for everyone. The main event was the beauty contest, of course, and this year all three elder girls had been entered. It was Susan's first year, whereas Ethel and Margaret had been placed on several occasions but had yet to be crowned the beauty queen. Margaret finished runner-up last year, which was the highest anyone in the Hughes family had achieved. The Stoney family had had a run of beauties for years and years, dating back to his grandpa's day, and Margaret had spent all year preening herself for the big event, believing that this year the crown was hers.

"Oh you look beautiful girls," Florence beamed as Susan and Ethel descended the stairs in all their finery. "Where's Margaret?" Florence asked concerned.

"She isn't coming," Ethel said forlornly.

"What!" Florence exclaimed in disbelief. She hastened past the girls and up the stairs into their overcrowded room. "Margie what's wrong love?" asked Florence.

"Go away I look awful Mam," Margaret's muffled voice sounded from under the bedclothes.

"I'm sure you don't, let's see," said Florence kindly.

"Look!" Margie shouted as she pointed to a huge hard lump under her skin. "I've got a boil!" Florence looked at the big red lump emerging under her eldest daughter's chin and had no answers.

"We'll ask your Anty Aggie what she thinks, she's always got a solution for everything," stated Florence.

"Not this one she's not!" Margaret sobbed.

Florence raced down the stairs and made a beeline for Alfie.

"Alfie!" she said as she shook him firmly. "Run round to your Anty Aggie's for me there's a good lad." Alfie looked horrified at the request.

"No chance you getting me round there, not after what Kim did to Clive!" Alfie said.

"Well I can't send Clive can a, he's terrified and girls will only go and get their sens ditched if I send them," Florence snapped. "Now get your sen round to Aggie's and stop moaning," she ordered.

"I'll go Aunty Florrie, I can run quicker than Alfie anyway," Clive said quietly, hoping to redeem himself a little.

"Oh Clive are you sure you'll not be too frightened of dog?" cooed Florence.

"I'll be fine, honest," Clive replied, only too keen to please in any way that he could now.

"OK well if you're sure," Florence said glaring disappointedly at Alfie and then made her way back up the stairs to tend to a wailing Margaret. Clive smiled smugly at Alfie and then sped out of the door and round to the house he had quickly abandoned only a few days before.

On his way round to Aggie's house, Clive had decided that he would just open the door quickly and run inside. He knew that if he dwelled on things, he was bound to lose his nerve.

"Gerald, where's Aggie?" Clive panted, as he burst through into the front room. Kim instantly growled at the sound of her foe's voice and Clive backed away timidly, as his fears were rekindled. Kim was not in the best of moods. She had a big day today and was being groomed within an inch of her life in preparation for it. Gerald, still angry with Clive, enjoyed watching his elder cousin squirm, he knew that Clive felt guilty for his actions earlier in the week and he was more than happy for him to receive the consequences.

"Did you want me Clive?" Aggie's voice echoed from the parlour. Trembling like a leaf, Clive stepped further into the house so Aggie could hear.

"Aunty Florrie needs you urgently, she said for you to come quickly," Clive said quietly.

"Okey-dokey, I'll be right with you," replied Aggie.

"Is Kim in the show again this year?" Clive asked tentatively. Gerald stopped brushing Kim and looked up at his frightened cousin. He thought how brave he was being by not running away like Alfie would and gave Clive a little more respect in his eyes.

"Yeh she's in best in show first and then dog's agility time trial straight after," Gerald replied.

"We all know she's the fastest dog in Nottinghamshire and she looks smart enough to win best in show, so long as she doesn't roll in any cow poo again this year, eh!" said Clive chuckling, trying to raise a smile from his cousin. "It was really funny, wasn't it Gerald?" Clive continued. "Do you remember the rancid smell and all the judges' faces when Kim paraded up and down clouded in eau de poo?" he encouraged.

"Well I'm keeping tight rein on her this year, I can tell you," Gerald said tugging at her leash. "She'll not be making me look daft again," he remarked, feeling annoyed that his cousin was having yet another joke on him.

"Come on then Clive, give us hand round ta Florrie's," Aggie interrupted sensing tension between the two boys. "Are you staying here Gerald?" Aggie quizzed, as she reached for Clive's supportive arm.

"Yeh best off staying where it's dry, dunt want to risk her getting filthy again. You know what she's like!" Gerald said scowling at Clive.

"All right sees you later then, when I've sorted out whatever's up with our Florrie. I'll be back to fix up Mae's baby bonnet," Aggie replied, leaving the house.

"Goodness gracious me Clive, I can hear them shouting and screaming from here," Aggie remarked as they turned the corner into Richmond street. Clive gingerly opened the door to the Hughes household to be faced with the hysterics of his female relatives. The noise was ear splitting. Margaret was still crying and sobbing, Florence was yelling at everyone to be quiet and Josie was chanting, "I'm going to win", over and over again. Eileen, in desperation, had immersed herself in an operatic song and was singing badly along to the gramophone and Susan and Ethel were squealing in high-pitched voices while Alfie chased them around the sitting room. It was bedlam!

Without a second thought, Aggie inhaled a deep breath stuck two fingers in her mouth and let out a piercing wolf whistle which stopped everyone in their tracks. The noise stopped instantly and everyone turned to see Aggie standing with her hands on her hips in the doorway.

"Right then, now I've got your attention," Aggie said calmly. She bent down to Josie's eye level and smiled kindly at her. "Why dunt you go out back and chant that lovely little tune so that everyone can hear you!" she said encouragingly. Thrilled at the idea of an even bigger audience, Josie trotted off instantly.

"Alfie stop chasing them pretty ladies and go help your Uncle Alan set up stall, I'm sure there'd be a bob or two in it for you," Aggie said. Noticing Clive's disappointment at not being offered the same opportunity, she quickly extended the same offer to him. "You too Clive, I'm sure he'd appreciate the help!" With the prospect of cash in their pockets the boys were off like a shot.

"Eileen, I think you should perhaps gargle a little salt water, you were starting to sound a bit croaky when I come in and we dunt want you to lose out to Betty Hargreaves again do we!" Aggie said trying to sound concerned. Eileen turned off the record instantly and hastened to the medicine cabinet in search of a remedy.

Now that the room was silent again, Aggie turned her attention to Margaret, who was now curled up on the living room sofa.

"Oh come on Mags it can't be that bad!" Aggie cooed as she approached Margaret's defeated frame.

"Oh Anty Aggie I'm so ugly!" Margaret muffled a reply.

Aggie raised her eyebrows at Florence, who in turn anxiously bit her bottom lip and then mouthed, "She's got a boil!"

"Come on let's take a look at it then girl," Aggie soothed.

"There's no point, there's nowt you can do!" Margaret retorted. Aggie turned to look at Florence for clarification. Florence gritted her teeth and nodded her head and Aggie new instantly that she had her work cut out.

"Move your hands then chicken, I can't see through your fingers," Aggie moaned as she tried to prise Margaret's fingers from her swollen chin.

Margaret slowly peeled back her fingers to reveal a bulbous red boil on the underside of her pretty little chin.

"OK!" Aggie said staring into her niece's tear-stained face. "This is what we're going to do. Beauty contest isn't tilt later, so that'll buy us some time, OK? Florrie get me some ice to take swelling down and make sure you cover it in flannel or you'll burn her skin," she ordered firmly. Florence bustled into the kitchen and quickly came back with the wrapped ice.

"Here you are love," Florence voiced anxiously. Margaret wistfully took the ice and applied it to the lump on her face.

"Florrie, do you still have some of our Mam's old face powder?" Aggie asked as she stroked Margaret's cheek comfortingly.

"Maybe, I'll go and check," Florrie replied as she rushed off to rummage in the kitchen drawers.

Seeing that Ethel and Susan's handsome appearances was not helping Margaret's mood or confidence Aggie saw the need to get them out of the house for a little while.

"Girls," Aggie said as she turned to Ethel and Susan. "Nip back to mine and fetch me our Mae's bonnet and bring it here will you please!"

"Oh no Anty Aggie, you were making that for baby," Margaret sobbed guiltily.

"I think you need it more today me darling," Aggie said as she gently patted her young niece's hand.

"Thanks Anty Aggie," she replied touched by her kindness.

"What about the dog and our outfits Aggie?" Susan remarked rather selfishly concerned for her own chances in the competition.

"Oh it's all right, we'll give our Gerald a shout for we go in, it'll be fine you'll see," Ethel responded, unperturbed by anything.

"No need to rush back. Be a while for I need bonnet. Got to get swelling down and make-up on first anyhow," Aggie encouraged, as she felt that Margaret needed the space.

"Here you are Aggs," Florence chimed.

"Oh that's brilliant Flo. If it can cover me Mam's black whiskers for 20 years I'm sure it can cover her boil," Aggie said wiggling her fingers under her nose. The sisters chortled at the memory of their incredibly hairy mother, but Margaret squirmed at the thought of having a moustache, which made them laugh even more. "See! Could be worse eh!" Aggie remarked enjoying her niece's reaction. "You could have had to shave twice a day like our Mam! That's better," Aggie smiled, as Margaret's face started to smirk. "We'll have you right as rain and ready to take on Grace Stoney in no time!" Aggie said encouragingly.

When the girls and Gerald returned from Aggie's house, a transformation had taken place. The endless ice packs had done their job and Grandma Daly's magic whisker powder had helped disguise the redness on Margaret's lovely face. Her long dark hair had been teased into beautiful tousling ringlets around her shoulders and down her back and she donned a pretty lemon dress with white lace trimming, which pinched in, to emphasise her tiny waste and slim figure. She was a picture.

"Wow! Gerald said, as he entered the front room for the first time that day. "You look right nice Maggie." Aggie smiled at him appreciatively as she took from him, the dainty bonnet she'd made so delicately for baby Mae. She held it gently on the back of Margaret's head.

"She'll look a picture once I've trimmed it with this," Aggie said, waving a lemon ribbon to match Margaret's dress. "We'll tie bow around chin so it will hide the problem completely, what do you think?" remarked Aggie, as she glanced at the other two girls.

"I think we have a winner!" Susan smiled meekly.

"I think we could have a clean sweep this year," Eileen cried, hugging Susan and Ethel supportively.

"Right, me job is done here for now, so I'm off to get me sen changed," Aggie said standing to attention, "because Alan's got schedule all laid out as usual, so I'd best get cracking," Aggie said chuckling to herself.

"Thanks so much Anty Aggie, you're wonderful," Margaret said squeezing her tightly.

"You're welcome sweetheart, I'll have your bonnet ready for competition and as you've only a little head it might well win two prizes today, coz I'll not have to adjust it for our Mae," replied Aggie.

"We'd better get move on too, or we'll miss all the fun. I have a feeling that we're going to have a good day today," Florence chirruped, as she ushered the rest of the family into action. Josie emerged from the kitchen, brimming with excitement holding her cake tin firmly in her small grasp.

"I'm ready," she chimed.

"Come on then poppet," Eileen said as she tried to retrieve the pie from Josie, "let's get that pie of ours to the stall before our luck changes eh."

"No Mummy I'm carrying the pie!" Josie scoffed. "It's my pie and I won't drop it if that's what you're worried about!"

"No, no, not at all sweetie!" Eileen said calmly. She knew better than to cross Josie, when she had her official business head on. "Come on then little lady let's see if we can get the best spot on the stall, for YOUR pie!" Eileen said winking at Florrie. The twosome skipped out of the door, neither able to contain their excitement and made their way down the hill towards the village green. Gerald, who still had a tight leash on Kim, quickly followed them flanked by Susan and Ethel, with Douglas in the knapsack on his back.

The second Saturday fete had grown in size every year since its formation and this year the local council had surpassed everyone's expectations. The village green had been transformed into a wonder of excitement. As the family passed through its gated entrance, they sighed at the volume of stalls, which bordered the park. Each had its own bright seaside canopy to protect the local produce from the burning summer sun. Centre stage to it all was the arena, which was dedicated mostly to the animal competitions. The horses were the most exciting to watch, as they charged up and down while their riders clung on for dear life. The dog's agility event always pulled in a crowd, but it was the best in show that the local families favoured the most, as every year they groomed their pet pooches and walked them out in the hope that they'd be crowned top dog in the village.

A new stage had been constructed this year, with a three-tier podium for the beauty contests, each dressed with magnificent flower arrangements. As there was such fierce rivalry in the baking competition, a special white marquee had been erected to house it and the local constabulary had been brought in to guard the variety of sponges, tarts, pies and pastries on offer. The event had been flooded with entries this year, due to the winner having direct entry into the 10 year national event, which had the benefit of a £100 cash prize.

Florence surveyed the area in search of people she knew and when she saw Lesley Osbourne bustling around the beauty stand, her heart sank, for she knew that Lesley only flounced around things when she had a vested interest in it.

"I see she's involved this year then," Florrie gestured as she nudged Aggie's arm.

"Well her niece, Arabella, is in competition, so she's going be isn't she!" Aggie remarked unsurprised.

"She's a real beauty!" Margaret sighed. Momentarily Florence felt despair, she'd spent all morning doing all she could to restore her daughter's confidence and now Lesley had thrown yet another spanner in the works. Was there no end to that woman's scheming to get everything her own way, she thought angrily.

Florence wasn't one for getting too involved, but she did know everyone, after all she'd lived in the village all her life. She knew people too; surely she could pull a few strings to aid her daughter in her quest. Florence wasn't about to cheat or manipulate, it wasn't her style, but letting Lesley destroy her daughter's confidence was not something that she was going to let happen.

Once again, Florence scoured the village green, but this time in search of influential people she knew. She saw PC Joyce guarding the cake stall and smiled as she was guaranteed his support, of that she was certain. Amongst the ladies collecting the cakes and pies in the marquee she noted Mrs Johnson and

Florrie smirked to herself. Mrs Johnson had been an adversary long before Lesley Osbourne had descended on her territory, thanks to Clive and his antics, so there was definitely no allegiance there. She scanned the faces amongst the stalls and her gaze fell on Alan. He was busy setting up his stall with Clive and Alfie dutifully by his side. She watched in admiration, as her brother-in-law easily made conversation with his co-workers and customers. Alan had such a relaxed manner with people, without getting too involved, and everyone liked him. She couldn't help feeling a little envious of his natural networking ability. It was a skill that she had once had and yet events in her life had left her bruised and lacking in confidence.

"Come on Florrie, I've got an idea," Aggie grinned, almost reading her sister's thoughts. Florrie leaned in tight and the two sisters bounded over to the local brass band, where Grandpa Hughes was proudly tuning his trumpet. "How about a bit of Glenn Miller, Grandpa," Aggie shouted. Florrie beamed as the musical sounds of '*In the Mood*' filled the arena. "Hey Margaret do you remember this one?" Aggie teased.

"What does she mean?" Susan asked intrigued.

"Oh it were nowt just had a couple of dances with an American soldier that's all," said Margaret.

"Really?" Susan said enthralled.

"Yes really," Margaret blushed.

"Not everyone gained the affections of the Yanks though did they eh Mags!" Aggie winked as she nodded towards the beauty contest stage.

"No they dint," Florrie smiled triumphantly as she watched Lesley scuttle over to Arabella who'd heard the music and instantly started to get upset.

"What happened Margaret?" Susan whispered seeing Arabella's reaction.

"It were only a bit of fun, but he did choose me over few other girls," Margaret said gesturing towards the stage.

"Did he want you to go back to America with him?" Susan enquired enthusiastically.

"No I were only 17 at time, but he were lovely and he did give me this before he went home," Margaret said as she unbuttoned her dress slightly to produce a long chain, which hung around her neck.

"Wow Margaret, he must have really loved you!" Susan beamed as she spotted a man's gold signet ring hanging at the bottom of the chain. "Doesn't that mean you're his girl when a boy gives you his ring Aunty Florrie?" Susan said spinning to ask.

"He fell hook, line and sinker for our Mags, I can tell you," Florrie replied. Margaret shyly placed the treasure back inside her dress and smiled modestly at her mum. Florence flashed a smile back at her eldest daughter pleased that her confidence was once again restored and thankful that she had such a treasure in Aggie.

Feeling now that her allies were growing in number, Florence beamed as she watched Alan, as animated as ever, come trotting across the field with Clive and Alfie in tow.

"Right then gang," he said whilst rubbing his hands together. "I have itinerary here and Gerald's up first with Kim in best in show," Alan said watching Gerald pat Kim proudly.

"We'll have to meet you there," Eileen said, starting to panic a little, as the sun beamed down on to the prize apple pie.

"Good luck Gerald," Josie chimed, as she walked steadily towards the marquee, clutching the warm pastry in her small hands.

"Thanks Jose, good luck to you an all," Gerald called after her. He slipped his knapsack off his back and handed it to Aggie. "Take care of him for me Anty Aggie," he said as he handed her his bag.

"Don't worry he'll be safe with me love," Aggie said smiling at Gerald.

"Come on Kim let's go and win our sens a prize," Gerald said as he bounded over to the stage,

The best in show did not involve much. They just had to trot up and down past the judges and look the best they could. Kim was a fabulous looking dog with the right height and posture and Gerald had ensured that she was well groomed for the event with her coat shining beautifully in the morning sun. Gerald knew that she was a fine figure of a dog, but worried that her poise would let her down. She had behaved impeccably all morning and avoided rolling in anything which smelt or stuck to her fur. He was confident that if she could just hold on for ten minutes more, she'd win her first trophy.

"And now we have Tabatha, she is three years old and last year's runner–up," the announcer boomed over the loudspeaker. "Tabatha is a long-haired Yorkshire terrier, doesn't she look glamorous, let's give our first contestant a warm welcome!" The crowd cheered as the tiny pooch paraded proudly in front of the judges. One by one the dogs were flaunted by their owners. All kinds of different breeds had entered the competition and each performed their role with grace and composure.

"The last entry is Kim the Alsatian, doesn't she look smart!" the announcer said enthusiastically. Gerald was hopeful that this year they might win a prize, as he had been training her all year. Kim, being an intelligent dog, was averse to being told what to do. Obedience was not something she particularly enjoyed, but if she was in the mood, there was no dog better. Gerald looked up to the sky and prayed that today she was in the mood, if she wasn't, then all hell could let loose.

Beaming with pride, Gerald paraded his well turned out dog in front of the five prestigious judges. Kim, enjoying the attention, trotted dutifully off her lead and obeyed Gerald's commands to sit and stay and so her first walk by was a triumph. Gerald couldn't believe how well behaved she was.

"Just one more run by girl and it's in the bag," Gerald whispered to Kim.

Slowly, Gerald clipped Kim back on her leash and guided her in a circular motion to face the other way in preparation to make their final pass. Directly following the best in show was the agility event and in an aim to get things running on time, the games makers were already setting up the obstacle course. Gerald hadn't seen this transition taking place and was unperturbed by it, but his partner had taken a great deal of interest in it. Gerald sensed Kim's excitement and pulled on her leash.

"Kim heel," he commanded to keep her under control, but Kim had other ideas and wanted to play. Suddenly her pace began to quicken from a brisk walk into a quick trot.

"NO KIM!" Gerald yelled, still clinging on to Kim's leash, but there was no stopping her. Kim was determined to have her fun and was getting very excited. Gerald dug his heels into the moist grass and pulled with all his might, but Kim was a strong dog and met his resistance with equal strength. The duo, were clenched in a battle of tug of war right under the disapproving eyes of the judges. An almighty cheer came from an amused crowd as the duo battled for supremacy, but Gerald proved to be the weaker contestant and Kim was free at last.

Gerald shamefully lifted his head from the ground where he had landed in dismay. He cringed as Kim rampaged through the newly set-up obstacle course; hid his eyes behind his splayed fingers as she weaved her way energetically through the vertical poles and raced over the ramps with athletic finesse. The games makers charged in to impede her, but this just added to her pleasure. She was having the time of her life and there was no stopping her. When she'd completed the entire course with such ease, she stood still in her tracks and surveyed the area around her. Gerald, who had risen to his feet by now, made one last attempt to regain control.

"Kim," he called and to his amazement she responded immediately by bounding across the arena in his direction. A sigh of relief passed over everyone's lips, but their joy was premature. Kim, who was within inches of Gerald's grasp, had spotted something else of interest to her and she made her way to the judges' table.

Frantically, Gerald stared at the judges' table in search of what could be so interesting.

"Oh no, Kim! No!" Gerald hissed, as he saw her purposely climb the slope of the stage and softly pad up on to the judges' table. She passed Lady Furnish in her fashionably large summer hat, sniffed at the bald head of her husband the Lord Mayor and skimmed nonchalantly past Mr Winterbottom, the old school headmaster. Kim waivered when she reached the village doctor but her interest fell on to the vicar.

Reverend Eastwick looked stunned as Kim stopped directly in front of him and peered into his bewildered eyes. She pressed her wet nose firmly against his and stared at him momentarily. Then with gentlest of motions, she tilted her head with her mouth just a little ajar towards the top of the reverend's head and carefully closed it on to the reverend's hair. Feeling the large dog's hold, the reverend quickly clasped his hands on top of his head. He had thick ginger hair, which was groomed to perfection and never seemed to move out of place, it was his prize possession and everyone knew it.

The entire village watched as Kim revealed the truth behind the ginger mane. She was not aggressive in her actions; in fact her motions were quite delicate. Kim tugged gently at the ginger mop as if requesting permission to do so from its owner. Beads of sweat were beginning to slip down the reverend's face now and his co-panel members sat back in horror as slowly, his carroty head of hair slipped off his head, down on to his glasses and slid off the end of his nose to reveal a shiny white boald crown with a snitch of ginger protruding out of the front of his head.

Once in possession of the brightly coloured wig, Kim launched herself off the stage and proceeded to race around the arena violently shaking the reverend's toupee as she went for the entire crowd to see. The reverend, already humiliated, saw no reason to maintain his dignity any longer and charged after her. The escapade proved a real crowd-pleaser as the games makers and local police force joined in too. Their pursuit only gave Kim more pleasure as she sidestepped the constabulary, knocking some into the apparatus and toppled any prospective captors in her wake into the Union Jack bunting.

The officials were beginning to feel defeated in their quest, when from amidst the crowd, came a booming voice which made Kim stop dead in her tracks. Guiltily, she turned towards an approaching Uncle Alan and cowered.

"Drop it!" he commanded and Kim dutifully placed the reverend's hairpiece on the grass in front of her. Alan picked up Kim's trailing lead and shortened its length to restrict her, and retrieved the soggy ginger wig from the ground. The reverend, who was approaching quickly, grabbed the hairpiece from him and looked at it in dismay. "I'm right sorry Reverend. What more can I say?" Alan said apologetically. The reverend said no more on the subject and Alan headed in Gerald's direction. Kim as ever was delighted to see him and jumped up enthusiastically only to be fiercely restrained by Alan. "DOWN!" he bellowed.

"Sorry Uncle Alan," Gerald winced, afraid of what his uncle would have to say to him.

"Oh don't worry lad, it weren't your fault and anyway did anyone expect anything less," he said offering a gentle smirk.

"Gerald are you OK sweetie?" Aggie gasped as she finally reached them.

"Yeh I'm OK," Gerald replied. "But I doubt she'll be able to enter agility competition now will she?"

"No love, they've already told me she's been disqualified. I don't think she's cut out for this sort of thing, do you?" smiled Aggie with laughter behind her watery eyes.

"No, but she were funny, weren't she!" Gerald grinned as he looked at his favourite relatives.

"Oh she's a card alright," his Uncle Alan agreed with a consoling arm around Gerald's shoulders. The threesome walked off acknowledging the crowd, who, much to the reverend's disgust, showed their appreciation with rapturous applause.

"What's next then?" Florence asked as she rolled up some of the shredded bunting.

Alan checked his list and proclaimed, "Our Josie's next. Come on, judging will be over by now!" In the distance Clive and Alfie were already waiting anxiously by the white marquee.

"Come on they're just about to announce the winner and look who they've asked to give out the prizes!" Clive giggled at the irony.

The dog's agility contest had coincided with the baking competition and so Eileen and Josie were shocked to see the entire family piling into the marquee, but Florence mouthed that everything was OK so they refocused their attentions on the judge. This year's head judge, in the absence of the butcher who had died only last week, was the delighted local baker, Mr Ganley, as he always thought it should have been his domain anyway.

"This year's winner," he grinned, "I am delighted to announce goes to a master baker indeed. They have produced a remarkable pie which not only equals, but dare I say, surpasses the culinary talents of the nine-time winner. No offence taken I assume Mrs Johnson," he scoffed.

Lorna Johnson smiled meekly back through gritted teeth. "Oh none taken Mr Ganley, none taken!"

"Well then with no further ado, this year's winner for her wonderful apple pie is Josie Challender! Let us give the little girl an enormous round of applause," he announced, clapping loudly. The tent erupted with whoops of joy and loud handclapping. "Mrs Johnson, if you could do the honours please," the baker egged. Josie dusted down her dress, turned to grin at her family and made her way towards the old lady. Mrs Johnson was not pleased that a mere child had been given such an accolade, but nevertheless, she performed her duty, despite Josie having to virtually prise the silver trophy from Lorna's mean little fingers.

"Well done child," Lorna said reproachfully. Josie stopped and before she accepted the award she turned and looked at Clive, who nodded his approval.

"Thank you," said Josie as she leaned forward to accept the prize. "We couldn't have done it without you!" she whispered and kissed the old lady on her cheek. Lorna pulled away in horror, as the realisation that her own apples had been used to bake the little girl's pie. Before Mrs Johnson could say anything Eileen was by her side.

"Did well didn't she Lorna, don't you think?" Mrs Johnson's face was crimson with rage.

"Yes with my stolen apples," she hissed. Eileen bent down so that she was face-to-face with the angry old lady, the tip of her nose almost touching the end of Lorna's.

"Come, come now Lorna. You shouldn't be too hasty with flippant remarks like that. After all, you wouldn't want anyone telling tales about you, now would you?" Lorna inhaled a deep breath, her eyes filling with fear and sadness. She recalled the contents of Eileen's letter and how much she genuinely knew about her past.

She had been puzzled how Eileen had come to know the events that she'd tried so hard to forget. It had all been so long ago and such a well-kept secret that she had always imagined no one would find out. She had built a new life for herself here in the village and couldn't risk anyone finding out what she had done. Lorna looked into the resilient hazel eyes of Eileen and sadly shook her head.

"I didn't think so," Eileen said confidently as she patted the little woman's shoulder. "Come on sweetheart let's go and enjoy the rest of that pie," Eileen chivvied leaving a remorseful Mrs Johnson in her wake.

"Revenge over now then?" Gerald asked as he came to stand next to Clive.

"Yes, with him it is," Clive said as he stared gleefully at a bewildered Mr Johnson being browbeaten once again by his tiny wife. "Truce," said Clive offering his young cousin his hand to shake.

"Truce," said Gerald accepting his gesture, believing that Clive really did mean it this time.

"So what's next Uncle Alan?" Gerald said laughing at his Aunty Aggie chanting and dancing with excitement with Josie in her arms.

"Oh it's a big one... Beauty contest!" Alan replied. Margaret, Ethel and Susan started to giggle excitedly and quickly made their way out of the marquee and headed towards the stage again. The girls collected their numbers from the judges' table and made their way up the steps to the stage, to join all the other young ladies already lined up ready for the competition. Amongst the contestants, were several local girls and one or two from outside of the village.

Margaret side glanced at her competition, as she walked by the other competitors already standing on the stage. All the girls looked lovely in their Sunday best outfits, which had been smartened up with ribbons and petticoats. First in line was Grace Stoney, who had won for the last few years. Margaret acknowledged Grace with a small smile, she knew her well. They had been best friends for years before the annual rivalry had taken over. Margaret had always felt ashamed and more than a little sad that the competition had cost them their friendship.

She continued along the line passing some girls she'd never seen before and others she knew only by sight and followed the directions of one of the judges to take her allocated place at the end of the row. Margaret adjusted her bonnet, ensuring that it was still covering her boil and as she did so she glimpsed at her rival to her left. It was Lesley Osbourne's niece, Arabella; as usual she was dressed in her immaculate expensive-looking clothes. She never failed to look anything but polished. She, like her aunty, radiated wealth and glamour, which made Margaret feel a little embarrassed to be wearing only a handmade dress in comparison. Despite this Margaret made the effort to speak to her.

"Is this your first contest?" Margaret whispered kindly. Arabella turned and stared at Margaret.

"What's that on your head?" Arabella retorted snobbishly.

"Me Anty made it for me!" Margaret replied solemnly as she fidgeted uncomfortably with her bonnet.

"Makes you look stupid," Arabella replied as she snootily flicked her long sun-kissed hair in Margaret's face. Margaret was momentarily hit by a pang of hurt and self-doubt, but then Susan and Ethel nestled in between them and their excitement took over.

One by one, the girls paraded in front of the judges, twirling around and smiling excitedly, each girl receiving a massive cheer as they curtsied to the crowd. The competition was about beauty inside and out and all the contestants had to be interviewed as well. The Reverend Eastwick had been given this task. Despite his capers with Kim earlier in the day, the reverend was a proud man and with the modicum of self-respect he had left and with his toupee now securely realigned he dutifully climbed the stage to take up his role.

The reverend walked along the line of girls and one by one, asked them a few simple questions. After several giggly and girlish responses, it was Margaret's turn to respond to the reverend.

"And last but by no means least, we have one of our long-standing contestants, Margaret Hughes," the reverend said moving into the empty space adjacent to Margaret. "Margaret, in your opinion, what do you think it takes to win a beauty contest?" the reverend asked, holding out the microphone to hear Margaret's answer. Margaret had listened attentively to the responses that her opponents had made to the reverend's similar questions and had cringed at the vanity of some of the contestant's answers.

Being last in the line she'd had plenty of time to think about her response. In the past she had always believed that the winner had always been chosen on her looks, but having listened to some of the beautiful girls awful responses, she was beginning to believe that it wasn't necessarily the case. Margaret cleared her throat and smiled politely at the reverend.

"Well Reverend, I think that beauty is more than just what you look like or how well you dress," she said tilting her head unconsciously towards Arabella.

"Interesting Margaret," the reverend schmoozed glancing up at her glamorous bonnet.

"I mean," Margaret continued, adjusting her chin strap. "You can look beautiful on outside without being beautiful on inside."

"I agree," the reverend smiled. "Do you think it's possible to have both Margaret?" asked the reverend.

"I think so. Take me friend Grace here. She's won competition for last couple of years. Not only is she very pretty, she's the nicest person I know and I can see now, why she always wins," Margaret said smiling at a blushing Grace.

"What about you Margaret?" the reverend egged, "Do you think you have both?"

"Oh I don't know Reverend. I try real hard to be as kind as a can and me Anty Aggie's done a good job of covering up me flaws today," she said tapping the bow on her chin. "But am not sure I could say I were beautiful in either respects."

"Thank you Margaret, real food for thought," the reverend said appreciating her manner and her beauty.

While the judges went to choose their finalists, the girls chatted amongst themselves and much to Margaret's delight Grace approached her.

"Thanks for that Margie, it were right nice of you," Grace beamed.

"It's all right Grace," Margaret said shyly. "It's true you are the nicest person I've ever met, Grace."

After much deliberation the judges chose their top three and put Ethel in third place for the third year running. Grace was placed second and despite topping the podium in first place, Margaret felt for the first time, that the competition didn't really matter. She had mended the rift between Grace and herself and that had made her happier than anything.

The successes continued throughout the day. Aggie was thrilled that the bonnet turned out to be a lucky charm, as Mae won the bonniest baby competition as well. Susan, after sulking for a short while, regained enough composure to enter and win the talent contest and made her second-placed mum very proud of her beautiful singing voice. Grandpa Hughes had been delighted when he won the top raffle prize of a crate of real ale and Clive and Alfie cleared up on the skittles and coconut shy stalls.

The final event of the day was the tug of war and Alan was determined that the family winning streak against the Gage family was not going to be broken. The women in the family gathered round and laid out a picnic blanket, in preparation for their cream teas, while Alan counted up the men and boys for his tug of war team. The females laughed as he frantically raced across the green with Kim in one hand and his itinerary firmly clutched in his other.

"Where's Albert?" Alan shouted. "I bet he'll not make it, he should have been here ages ago!" he said starting to panic.

"Don't worry I'm sure he'll be here soon," Aggie cooed, taking Kim from his grasp and securely tethering her to the nearest tree.

"He should be here now!" said Alan tapping his wristwatch.

"He's here," Gerald yelped with glee as he saw Albert approaching, "and he's got James and Michael with him too!" Gerald screamed with excitement. "What are you doing here?" he asked as he raced excitedly towards his old friends, but James and Michael looked weary.

"We are going to live with Uncle Albert from now on," Michael sighed. Gerald wanted to jump for joy that his friends were back for good but sensed that there was more to the story and perhaps now wasn't the time to talk about it.

"You can tell me all about it later then, when were done winning this tug of war eh!" Gerald said softly.

"Sorry we're late my friend! Did I miss anything?" Albert said, patting Alan on his back.

"Nowt really, only usual blast of them singing national anthem, for match," he said indicating towards the opposition.

"Wait until they hear what choral tunes we have planned for today," Albert smirked.

"Is everything OK?" Alan asked gesturing towards the two boys.

"Oh that's a story for another day and anyway we've got a tug of war to win!" Albert trilled.

Alan had watched how the Gage boys had grown over the year. He knew that without Billy and Charlie on the team it would be much weaker and if they stood any chance of retaining the tug of war crown, the new recruits had to be prepared. A week before the summer fete, Alan had organised daily training sessions to get them fit and ready for the event. It had proved to be a chore, what with Albert being away so much, but he never stopped believing that his team's diligence would pay off and they would once again be victorious.

"Right," Alan said, bringing his team into a group huddle. "Kick your shoes off and give them to the little women," Alan said gesturing to the girls, who ran to collect them. "No one's slipping this year!" he said scowling at Alfie.

"Opposition's bit tougher this year isn't it, Alan," Clive interrupted.

"Yeh few of Gage's lads look like they've grown a bit, so I agree we've got our work cut out," Alan acknowledged nodding his head. "So rub your hands in some of this," Alan said passing around a virtually empty old sandbag.

"What's this for Uncle Alan?" Gerald enquired.

"It's to keep your hands dry lad stop them sweating so you not slip and lose your grip on rope," he replied.

"What a perfectly splendid idea, Alan, I can see you've thought of everything this year!" Albert said congratulating his smart friend.

"Ah you know, not just a pretty face me," Alan laughed, pleased that his meticulous planning was being appreciated by someone.

"Right then lads," he said smiling to himself, "let's give them a blast of our new team chant and make it a good one, say it with me lads!" The six-strong team, all still huddled together, linked arms and bounced together, the men went first.

"OGGIE, OGGIE, OGGIE."

"Oi, oi, oi!" The boys responded equally as loud.

"OGGIE," came the response from the women.

"Oi," followed a tremendous response from all the team. "OGGiE, oi, OGGiE, OGGIE, OGGIE, oi, oi, oi." The team, turned to look at the Gage family.

"Oh dear," Alan said. "That's peed on their strawberries ain't it," he said smiling at their stunned reaction.

Despite not being the heaviest of the bunch, Alan set himself as the anchor-man, it was his position and no matter how big the boys were getting, while he was on the team it always would be. The rest of his team was traditionally set out, with the smaller boys at the front and the heavier men at the rear. The opposition was not so organised and it didn't take long for their incompetence to irritate Alan.

"Aggie," Alan shouted to his wife, across the arena. "Come and sort this lot out will you." Aggie dutifully trotted across to the other team, raising her hands to the appreciative cheers of the villagers. She had been asked to oversee the contest, due to her excellent organisational skills and fair team spirit. After a few moments Aggie had put the opposition in a suitable order and under the beady eye of her husband ensured that the flag was directly over the line, so that no team had an advantage.

Grandpa, who had volunteered to commentate on the match again, felt relaxed as he prepared to relay the event to his captive audience. He'd always remained composed in previous years as he prided himself on being the consummate professional and despite the Hughes family always winning no one could accuse him of being nepotistic in his commentary. This year with Billy and Charlie gone the Hughes family had lost their long-standing advantage and Grandpa definitely knew that his relations were the under dogs. Despite Alan's determined and positive words that his team were still going to lift the trophy again this year, Grandpa had not been convinced and had prepared himself for an easy victory for the Gage family.

With the sound of the whistle, the teams were off. Both teams heaved with all their might. The Gage team launched an early attack and for a short while they had a small advantage. It seemed inevitable in the first few seconds of the tug of war contest that the Hughes family were going to be no match for the larger boys this year and that Grandpa was going to be right, but then the Hughes' team's pride kicked in and they found their spirit. With the flag pulled back to the centre mark, the Hughes team saw their opportunity to strive hard for victory over their age-old nemeses.

The Hughes family dug their bare heels determinedly into the soft grass and Grandpa's chest swelled with pride as he saw the gleam of victory once again appearing in his team's eyes. He had become despondent when the Gage family had taken an early lead but now he had a real match to report on and for the first time that day he believed that maybe, just maybe they could win. Swallowing back his tears of joy Grandpa started his commentary.

"The lighter team seems to be gaining a bit of an advantage now, over the Gage family," Grandpa said hopefully. "Hughes family have certainly got a better grip with no shoes on," he continued excitedly. "Gage family, really struggling now, starting to slip all over place," he continued with a mocking tone, as he rose to his feet. "Yeh, the Hughes boys are gaining with every tug," he exclaimed as his voice quivered with enthusiasm. "Only a couple inches now and they've got them. I think they're going to do it! They are, they are, me boys are going to do it!" he yelped excitedly as he rapidly vacated his box and ran to within metres of the event, bellowing excitedly at the top of his voice. "Go on lads you're going to do it!" he shouted. "Bring it home lads," he yelled as he jigged up and down watching his team cruise over the finish line to victory. "Yes!" he cheered as the Hughes family launched their final tug to make the Gage family tumble like dominoes on to the ground in front of them. The crowd cheered as Grandpa youthfully jumped the rope and hotfooted it across the arena to join his family in their celebrations. Grandpa acknowledged his overexcitement by waving happily to the crowd. He had become very animated inside his commentary box, but his pure joy at seeing his family win had taken over and everyone loved it.

The fete drew to a close at 5.00 p.m., the stall keepers began to pack away their wares and the committee set to work taking down the decorations, marquees and stages which had been set up for the day. The hordes of village people, who had gathered together, cheerily made their way to the exit. The second Saturday had, once again, been a wonderful day for everyone who had got involved and the Hughes and Challender families were no exception. With their hearts full of joy, they gathered up their trophies and rosettes, folded away the picnic blanket and meandered across the village green towards their homes.

Gerald pulled his knapsack on to his back, its weight reassuring him that Douglas was still safely inside. He untied a sleeping Kim from the tree, no doubt exhausted from her frolics earlier in the day and handed the leash to his Uncle Alan. Flanked by his dear friends James and Michael he too strolled merrily across the village green. He wondered what could have happened in London to make Nottinghamshire their permanent home. He detected sadness behind their joy and hoped that they would be ready to tell him their story soon. For today, they had been happy and he didn't want to spoil it.

Gerald looked ahead of him and his eyes fell on his mother, gaily walking alongside Albert. She had been much happier of late since Albert had come back into their lives. He thought about his plans to talk to his mum about Douglas and his belief that Douglas could ease her pain, as he had his Aunty Aggie, but seeing her now with Albert he considered that perhaps she was on her way to recovery all by herself. He hitched up the knapsack on his shoulder and sauntered out of the gates towards his aunt's home, weary after the day's events.

Exhausted, Gerald climbed into bed, tucked himself in and pulled his knapsack up next to him. Douglas was still encased inside. Gerald lifted Douglas out and held him tightly, slowly he drifted off to sleep recollecting Kim's mischief and wondering what magic and mystery day 14 of his holidays would bring.

Day Fourteen
Letters for Mrs Hughes

Florence awoke refreshed in the morning, feeling for the first time since she had discovered that her husband had gone missing during the war, it was without a heavy heart. She had thoroughly enjoyed her day at the village fete and was particularly pleased to see the return of Albert. She had been concerned that his mysterious absences may mean that he was leaving the village for good and her heart had ached at the thought. Her brief conversation with him though, as they strolled across the village green the day before, had set her mind at ease.

She had been shocked to see James and Michael at his side but Albert had explained the reason why he had been away, during their walk. Albert's sister had passed away after suffering from pneumonia for some time and he had informed Florence that he was now their legal guardian. Albert had also told Florrie that he had had to keep travelling to London to fight for custody and it was only today that the authorities had agreed to release them into his care.

Florrie was of course sad for the boys, losing their mother in this way. Although she felt that it must have been devastating for them, she couldn't help feeling that they would have a better life with their uncle. She had no doubt that he would make a wonderful father, which is something they had never really had. Unlike Albert, his sister had made bad choices in her life, leaving her children fatherless and herself in ill health. Florrie thought of her own children growing up without their father and her thoughts turned to Gerald.

She felt proud of how he was turning out. Florrie had been worried for a while, with his constant lying, but since the start of the summer she had seen a positive change in him. His new cheery disposition had made her worry less and allowed her to be happier as well. Albert's return to their lives had had a huge influence on Gerald and she was thankful for that. Selfishly, she was pleased Gerald's two best friends had returned for good, not only did it mean that Albert would now be a constant in Gerald's life again she hoped that he would remain one in hers too.

Florrie washed and dressed and went downstairs to prepare breakfast for her sleeping brood. Her terraced house brimmed with her family and although she loved them dearly, she was glad that the Challenders were nearing the end of their summer vacation. She set to work in the parlour singing tunefully to the wireless when, she heard tapping at the front window.

"Coming," she chirruped. Behind the tapping, was the cheerful face of the local postman. In his right hand he waved a parcel and in his left, a letter. Excitedly, Florrie opened the door, the only post she had received recently were bills. "Morning Malcolm," she beamed.

"Got a parcel here for your Gerald! And a letter for you an all Florrie, both postmarked France!" he said curiously.

"Thanks Malcolm," she said kindly and closed the door clutching the brown paper parcel in one hand and the foreign looking envelope in the other. Florence never intended to be rude, but she often cut her conversations short with him as he was a nosey man who could be indiscreet with the information he became privy to. Florence placed Gerald's parcel on the kitchen table for him to open later, he was still sleeping at his Aunty Aggie's so she would pop it round after breakfast she thought. She traced her fingers over her name and address scribed in the most beautiful script on the envelope addressed to her. It was not handwriting that she recognised. Florence gently squeezed the plump envelope between her fingers, impressed with the quality and wondered who could have so much to say to her? She observed the unfamiliar French stamp in the top right-hand corner and turned it over in search of a return to sender's address, but nothing was written on the reverse.

Florrie placed the envelope face up on the table and boiled the kettle to make herself a cup of tea. She pulled out the dresser drawer in search of the silver letter opener she'd had as a wedding gift and placed it adjacent to the letter. After pouring herself a comforting brew she sat down expectantly at the table. She drew the strange letter towards her and slid the silver opener through the envelope to reveal its contents. Breathing deeply, Florrie opened the letter and began to read.

Bonjour Madame Hughes,

You do not know me, but I feel that I know you very well. This has been a very difficult letter for me to write and I hope that you do not find my correspondence impertinent or intrusive, as my words are well meant and written with the very best of intentions.

My name is Annivette Dumas and during the Second World War I was a nurse stationed at the military section of a hospital in Normandy. In the winter of 1940 a man was brought into my care. He was badly injured and had no recollection of who he was. As he didn't have any form of identification about his person when he was found, he could not be identified. I later discovered this man to be Charlie Hughes, your husband.

Gradually over time his injuries started to heal and you could see the life crawl back into his green eyes. At the end of the Second World War the military part of the hospital was closed and the patients were sent home to England. As he could not be identified, the air force did not know where to send him. Disinclined to be returned to the country of his birth without the true knowledge of who he was or where he belonged, he bravely chose to stay on in Normandy, in the hope that one day he would regain his memory and be able to return home to the life he knew before the war. With my help he gained employment as a carpenter and went on to build furniture and make wooden toys for children. He tried everything to regain his memory but nothing would trigger it. A year after the war had ended, he became resolved that it would be unlikely that he would regain his memory and had to accept that his past may be lost to him forever.

He was starting to rebuild his life here in France and it'd been the happiest I had seen him in all the years I'd known him. Having accepted that this was his new life now, he finally opened up to the idea of falling in love. After years of loving him so deeply, I was blessed that he chose me to share his new life with. We were content and earlier this year I fell pregnant with our first child. After a few months into my pregnancy Charlie began to have flashbacks to his former life and by the time I was six months pregnant, he had regained most of his memory.

Charlie, tortured with remorse, was determined to return to England to see his family and try to explain, the best that he could, where he had been all these years. When he told me that you were the love of his life, I shamefully felt jealous and angry. He talked about his big close family but in particular the son that he had never really got to know. Charlie felt desperately guilty that his son had grown up with no memory of his father and he so wanted to be reunited with him, to tell him that he had not been forgotten and that he loved him dearly. Madame I feared that I would lose him forever and so in a gesture of my true love for him, I revealed the secret that I had held so tightly since its discovery many years before.

Charlie was so angry with me when I showed him the unopened letter addressed to you. He couldn't believe that I had hidden such a clue to his past from him for all this time. In a rage he left. Several hours later the local police came to tell me that Charlie had been involved in an accident and had had a head-on collision. He was badly hurt in the accident and was hospitalised for two weeks.

During his stay in hospital, he became delirious with fever and for the first time since we first met my face became unrecognisable to him. He smiled brightly with his eyes tightly closed as he uttered his young son's name. Madame, I have to confess to you now, that my heart broke when it was not my face that Charlie sought when he opened his eyes, his words so loving and gentle. 'Florrie,' he echoed as he drifted in and out of consciousness.

Desperate to bring him back, I shamefully assumed the name as my own, but still my words weren't enough and he slipped away from me and into a place I didn't know. His fever worsened every day, as his crushed leg turned gangrenous. The doctors did their best and even amputated his leg to try and save him, but it was too late. Once he'd fallen into a deep coma, he never recovered.

I have always felt great shame that I never told Charlie that I found his letter to you in the lining of his flying jacket, but it is now that I am filled with the most regret. I knew instantly that the letter would lead him to his forgotten past. I realise now, it must have caused you torment over the years, not knowing if he was alive or dead and for this I am truly sorry. As I never had chance to say how sorry I was to Charlie I have done what I think he would have wanted me to do and I have enclosed his letter.

Charlie mentioned that you had fought before he left for the last time, but couldn't remember why. As you will see his letter still remains unopened, because I respected that his words were meant for your eyes only. I really do hope that the contents of the letter help to put those battles behind you.

I have also sent you a package, containing a gift for Gerald, which should arrive at the same time as this letter; Charlie had made this for his young son and intended to give it to Gerald when he saw him. I hope that my words have not caused you too much pain.

I want you to know that it wasn't until Charlie had given up all hope of remembering you, that he allowed me to become part of his life. Although I knew he was fond of me, I knew his heart belonged to another and that is why I have contacted the British air force to bring him home to be buried, as that is where he was dreaming of when he died.

I hope that you can find it in your heart to forgive me
Annivette

Florence read and reread Annivette's letter until her vision became so blurred by her tears that she could no longer see the words on the page. She had waited so long to hear any news from Charlie, but never expected this. For years she had lived with the hope that he would walk through the door fit and well. She had suffered in silence, the not knowing whether he was still alive or dead had been the hardest thing to bear and it had until recently, drained her of happiness.

As the years had passed, she had so desperately wanted to move on with her own life, but until this very moment, she'd couldn't because she was still his wife. Florence skimmed her eyes once more over Annivette's words, recalling the last day that she had seen Charlie. Annivette was right, they had quarrelled before he left. For all these years, she had lived with the regret of not settling things before he returned to battle and like Annivette, she felt she'd have to live with that guilt now forever.

Although she felt annoyed at this woman she didn't know, she understood her reasons. She too had loved Charlie so desperately once. Smiling she recalled how they met at the local dance. He had been romantic and attentive.

He had made her feel special with his adoring love letters and poetic words and she fell instantly for his charms. He was an upstanding member of the community and from a good family. He was the type of person her father had expected her to marry and so at 19 she did.

Charlie had never failed to write to her while he was away at war and dutifully she had replied to his letters. When she received no letter after his last visit, she began to worry. Despite his many faults, Charlie was not sulky by nature, always being the first to easily forgive when they had argued, so as time passed she feared the worst.

Florence reached inside Annivette's envelope and pulled out the second letter. The postmark on the stamp dated exactly one week after the day he had returned to the war. Lovingly she smoothed her fingertips over her faded husband's handwriting and breathed deeply. It was clear from Annivette's letter, that he had not recalled all the details of that fateful day in June 1940, as he had expressed nothing but love for her. Encased inside the letter she was holding in her hands, were his undisclosed feelings to her and her alone. She didn't know what she expected to find inside the seven-year-old letter but she hoped that he had forgiven her for her huge indiscretion, as unequivocally as he had their petty fights in the past.

The old grandfather clock chimed loudly striking the hour of eight. Florence wiped her tear-stained face, placed the two letters in her apron pocket, picked up Gerald's box and purposefully pushed her chair back under the kitchen table. Today was going to be a difficult day for all her family, she had a funeral to plan and she had to speak to Albert sooner rather than later.

"Is Gerald up Aggie?" Florence asked as she entered her sister's house.

"No he's still sleeping. He were right poorly in night with a fever and then shivering!" said Aggie.

"Why didn't you fetch me?" Florence replied annoyed.

"Because it were late and he's OK, honestly don't worry," she soothed. "You alright Florrie? You look really pale!" asked Aggie. Florrie didn't say anything she just reached inside her apron and handed her sister only the larger of the two envelopes and waited for her response.

Aggie accepted the letter and began to read. Her eyes too filled with tears, as the words rolled out in front of her. When she'd finished reading, Aggie closed the letter and reached for her sister's hand.

"Oh Florrie I am so sorry," she said comfortingly. "I don't know what else to say. It's such an awful thing to happen, when he was almost home."

"It's OK Aggie; I always expected to receive a letter telling me he were dead, but not like this. It were brave of Annivette to write me don't you think? I'm grateful that she's shared the part of his lifetime that were missing," Florence said smiling meekly.

"What about his letter to you, have you read that yet?" Aggie asked.

"Yeh," Florence nodded sadly. "Read it on way over here. There were things between Charlie and me that weren't settled and now they are," she said wistfully.

"I did wonder! But you can move on with your life now Florrie, I think you've mourned enough these last seven years don't you?" Aggie sympathised slipping her arm around her sibling's shoulders.

"Yes," Florence said sniffing back her tears. "The hardest part's going to be telling Gerald!" she sighed.

"What's going to be hard to tell me?" Gerald yawned, as he descended the stairs. Florence opened up her arms to her youngest child and embraced his young frame.

"You feeling any better? Anty Aggie said you'd been poorly in night," asked Florrie.

"Yeh, fete really wiped me out," he said, stroking an energetic Kim. "Feel OK now though Mam, honest." Tears welled up once again in Florence's eyes.

"Come and sit down Gerald, I've got summat to tell you." Gerald accepted his mother's hand and did as he was bid. He listened intently as she explained to him that his dad had died. That he had been coming home to them when he had been in an accident and that his injuries had eventually taken his life.

Gerald looked into his mother's teary blue eyes, as she explained that his father had been living another life in France for years. He listened, as she told him how he hadn't come home sooner, because he had lost all recollection of whom he was and where he was from. Gerald wished he could share his mother's pain, but his tears didn't come. He didn't know how to feel, as he didn't really know his father. He had no real bond with him, as he had only been very small when he left for the war.

Being bereft of the gift of two parents for as long as he could remember had always made him feel that he couldn't connect with his siblings, as he'd missed out on the bond that they had with their father. Until Douglas had come into his life, he had to admit he really didn't feel happy, but his life had changed that day. Gerald now had a joy in his life and a friendship like no other. He had shared emotions that he didn't know were possible and he had learned to trust again. Finding Douglas had brought Albert back into his life and had also helped his precious Aunty Aggie share in her grief. Gerald thought about his friend trapped inside the cocoon and at that moment wanted no more than to just be with him.

"I think I need to be on me own for a bit Mam," Gerald said.

"Oh that's OK, take your time love. It's a lot to take in all in one go," Florence nodded gravely. "Oh don't forget this," his mother said handing him the brown parcel. Gerald took the parcel from her and stared at the beautiful handwriting.

"Who sent it?" Gerald asked puzzled.

"A friend of your Dad's", Florence replied glancing nervously at Aggie. Gerald tucked the parcel under his arm and hastily made his way back up the stairs to his shared room.

He placed the parcel on the bed and grabbed his knapsack, which was lying strewn on the floor. Reaching inside he remembered that he'd taken Douglas out the night before and searched his bed for the stone-like object.

"I moved him sweetie," his Aunty Aggie smiled as she entered the room. "You was tossing and turning and throwing all them covers off, I thought it be for the best!"

"Where is he?" Gerald looked expectantly at his aunty.

"I put him in me room for safekeeping, but when I went to fetch him just now, this is all there were!" Aggie said handing Gerald a broken cocoon with the contents empty.

"He's hatched!" Gerald said excitedly racing into Aggie's bedroom. "Where is he?" Gerald said, as the fresh air blew in through the windows. Aggie stepped gently into the room and closed the open window.

"I'm so sorry Gerald but he's gone."

The tears that Gerald couldn't find when his mother had told him the news about his dad came in floods when he realised that Douglas had gone. Aggie had tried to console him but he had just shunned her affection, feeling angry that she had been careless leaving the window open. He tried to join his family at mealtimes, but food was tasteless to him today and the mournful atmosphere had just made him feel worse.

From the confines of his bedroom Gerald wondered where Douglas could be now. He had wanted so desperately to see how he had transformed and wondered whether in his new form he'd learn more from him. Bereft and alone once again, for the first time this summer, Gerald wasted the rest of the day sleeping. No one questioned his behaviour as everyone was solemn and each grieving for his dad in their own way. As he was not disturbed for the rest of the day, he just assumed that they thought he must be grieving for his dad too.

Day Fifteen
A New Beginning

Gerald woke with a heavy heart. His mother had told him last night, when she brought him some supper that they had heard that his father's body would be arriving in the morning. She'd made him aware that his Uncle Alan had arranged with the funeral directors, for Gerald's father to be buried the same day and had selected a plot at the cemetery on Florence's behalf. Aggie had gone with him, as it was the day that they had planned to see where their baby's ashes had been spread.

"Can I come in?" Gerald lifted his head from his pillow and peered towards the door. Albert stood solemnly in the doorway.

"Yep," Gerald said swinging his pyjama legs out of bed. Albert made his way towards his young friend and sat down next to him.

"How are you feeling?" Albert asked kindly. Gerald's eyes glazed over and he nestled into Albert's chest. "I heard about Douglas, your Aunty Aggie told me!" said Albert.

Gerald lifted his head to face Albert, "I have lost me Dad and Douglas all in one day!"

"I know Gerald, I know!" Albert soothed. "Gerald, I'm afraid that I have something that I have to tell you as well," Albert confessed.

Gerald pulled back in horror. "You're not leaving me an all, are you?"

"No, no, don't worry. James, Michael and me are here for good now," he said patting his arm comfortingly.

"What is it then?" Gerald quizzed.

"Did you ever wonder where I was when, when I went away for a while?" said Albert.

"Me Mam said you'd gone to look after your sister and that when she died you had to sign papers so that James and Michael could stay with you!" Gerald replied.

"That's partly true," he nodded. "But when I was in London, I also went to visit the British embassy," Albert said softly.

"The embassy? What for?" Gerald asked a little confused.

"I have been looking for your Dad Gerald," explained Albert.

"What made you go to embassy now, when he's been missing for all these years?" Gerald said, still puzzled. Albert removed his cap from his head and twisted it uncomfortably in his fingers.

"Do you remember when you first left Douglas in my care?"

"Yeh," Gerald nodded.

"Well that night, when I picked him up to place him in his new bed, because he'd grown so much, something magical happened," Albert smiled remembering the day. Gerald was not surprised to hear this, as he had always thought Albert knew more than he was telling him. "He spoke to me Gerald, in a voice I used to know so well." Intrigued Gerald listened closely.

"What did he say Albert?" Gerald demanded.

"His speech was by no means clear, but I could understand that he was hurt and needed to get home, I

215

didn't make the connection at first, but later, after the things you told me, I knew there was no doubt who he was!" Albert picked up the parcel that Gerald had received in the post the day before and handed it to Gerald. "I believe that your answer may be in here Gerald." Gerald held the parcel once again in his hands unsure what Albert meant. "Open it!" Albert urged.

Gerald tore off the brown paper to reveal a wooden box beautifully carved with the inscription 'For my son' inserted on the lid.

"Go on," Albert smiled. "It's OK." Gerald lifted the lid and inside, encased in a green leaf was a superbly painted toy. Gerald lifted the wooden carving out of the box and stared into its familiar bright green eyes.

"It's Douglas!" Gerald yelled. "But how did you know?" he said looking at Albert.

"When I saw your mum yesterday, she told me everything and when she mentioned that you'd received a parcel from your dad, something just told me it would be this. Your dad loved making you toys when you were a baby, I just guessed I suppose, that he'd chosen to visit you in the form of something that he'd lovingly made for you," explained Albert.

"It's hard to believe that all this time, my dad were Douglas," Gerald smiled.

"I guess he just so desperately wanted to see you. He had lost so much time while he had no memory of his past, that while he was dying his soul came to find you," Albert said sadly.

Gerald clutched the toy to his heart and tears welled up in his eyes. The memories of what he saw came flooding back to him. The young couple who were so happy and in love and the overwhelming sense of love which Douglas gave him.

The sterile and clinical white hospital beds and the horrendous fevers and faints he had experienced. Everything made sense to him now, he understood why he'd seen the things that he had. He had lived out his dad's last days with him and they would be memories that he would be able to treasure forever.

"His foot's not bleeding," Gerald pointed out.

"I guess that must have happened to Douglas when they amputated your dad's leg," Albert suggested.

"And look he's not wearing any goggles, either," Gerald mused.

"Oh yes," Albert said, examining the wooden toy. "Funny really, it's such an obvious clue, and yet we missed it!" Albert said smiling to himself. Gerald nodded, in agreement.

"What about me Anty Aggie and what she saw, though?" Gerald asked.

"I think I should let her explain that to you," Albert said kindly.

"Is there anything else that a need to know Albert?" Gerald quizzed. Albert looked hesitantly at Gerald, he so desperately wanted to tell him everything that his mother had confided in him, but he had agreed with Florence that now would not be the right time to tell him, so he pushed back his own feelings and focused on getting Gerald through the day.

"Like what?" said Albert.

"You love me Mam don't you Albert?" Albert tried hard to suppress his smile.

"Yes Gerald I do, very much. Do you think that would be OK?" Gerald looked at the green eyes of his wooden toy.

"I think my dad would have liked that!" he said.

Albert smiled faintly remembering what Florrie had read him from Charlie's letter and replied, "I hope so Gerald, I really do!"

As Albert left the room, it was only moments before Aggie entered. Gerald hadn't seen her since she had told him about Douglas.

"Can I come in?" she said softly.

"Of course you can," Gerald replied, still guilty for shunning her the day before.

"How are you feeling?" she asked caressing his hair. Gerald had hidden his wooden toy when Albert had left the room, as secretly as he had when Douglas was in his possession, but when Aggie came in he quickly pulled him out again.

"I feel OK, I think," Gerald said clutching his new toy.

"Was he in box?" Aggie smiled.

"Yeh," Gerald nodded.

"The resemblance is uncanny," she said admiring the caterpillar's red, white and blue stripes.

"You knew dint you? That Douglas were me Dad," Gerald said stroking the wooden caterpillar. Aggie held Gerald's free hand and squeezed it tightly.

"When I lost me baby, your mam struggled to give me the support I needed at time. It were guilt I suppose because she'd got you. I were always very close to your dad. Like I told you, he always tretted me like I were his kid sister, with me being so much younger than our Florrie. It sempt like he helped me so much with me grief, your Uncle Alan and I wouldn't have survived together without him," Aggie said thoughtfully.

"So were it me dad holding your baby, that day?" Gerald asked.

"Yeh Gerald it were. I dint want to say, in case I upset you but that day Douglas helped me to look forward in me life, instead of living in past all time. Now there's just one more thing I have to do and then everything will hopefully be OK."

218

Aggie patted Gerald on his knee and left him to get dressed into his Sunday best ready to join his family to attend his father's funeral. Florence had arranged for a small family church service first. Despite her reservations, she knew it would have been what Charlie wanted, with him coming from such a devout Catholic family.

Florence had looked around the church and found Albert's gaze. For years she had felt such guilt for loving him so deeply in the way that she did and later for doing him such an injustice. Florence had always wanted to tell him the truth about Gerald, but had feared his reaction. She had felt such love for him and had desperately needed to share her secret, but it wasn't until she'd read Charlie's letter and received his forgiveness that she had the strength to tell him. When Annivette's letter had arrived, she had felt so grateful to her for finding and sending her Charlie's letter, as its contents had given her the chance to move on with her life. She was thankful too, for Gerald's sake, that Charlie had no recollection of its contents when he died and that he still believed that she had been his one true love and that Gerald was his son.

As she watched her husband's coffin being brought into the church, she thought what a truly wonderful man he had been. In her heart she knew that she never truly loved him. Charlie was what her dad and family had wanted for her and he had, like they all said he would, made a good husband and father. In his last letter to her, he had told her that he knew that she had outgrown his love and that he accepted that she had fallen so deeply in love with Albert. He had asked for the chance to rekindle their love when he returned from war, but should he fail to come home, he believed Albert to be a fine and honourable man and knew that he would make her happy. Florence stared at the coffin as the priest read the Mass. She marvelled at her husband's capacity to forgive, despite his anger at how badly she had wronged him.

Albert smiled affectionately at Florence, his heart bursting with the love he had held in for all these years. He had lost his best friend seven years ago and today was the acknowledgement of that. He had welcomed the words which Charlie had written to Florence confirming his acceptance of their love, and although he had been shocked when Florence had told him that Gerald was his, he was thrilled to have a son of his own.

Albert had always felt a strong connection with the boy and come to love him dearly, but he knew that he would have to respect Florence's wishes not to tell Gerald the truth until she was ready, as much as it pained him to do so. Albert knew that it must have been difficult for Florence to live with her secret for so long and although he would take the secret to his own grave, he promised himself that he would spend the rest of his life making up for lost time and be the best dad he could be to Gerald. Content that he had tried to find his friend, when he believed Charlie to still be alive and satisfied that he had his blessing, he looked forward to a new beginning with his new wife and family.

Eileen caught sight of the two of them, unaware of the depth of their relationship. She had suspected that they had fallen in love some time ago and felt happy that they could finally be together after years of waiting for news of her brother. Her mind went back to the things she had to settle at home before she could start her own new life in North Nottinghamshire. Eileen had tolerated her husband's bullying when it had just affected her, but when Clive's antics this summer had exposed her husband's treatment of her child, enough had been enough. PC Joyce had offered for them all to move into the police house, when she'd confided in him at the fete, but Eileen wasn't certain it was a relationship she wanted to reignite and didn't want to hurt him again if she wasn't sure.

Florence had thankfully offered her home for Eileen and her family to take refuge in, as after she and Albert were married they would be moving into Header Vale Farm. It had been Aggie who had suggested it, she'd suspected for a while that things hadn't been right between Vic and Eileen and was quick to find a solution to her problem when Florence had announced their news. Eileen had accepted the gesture as she found the idea of living in her brother's home comforting.

She had been both shocked and amused to learn that Albert was the Osbourne's landlord, as Lesley had always given the impression that she owned the farm. At first she had questioned why Florence didn't take the opportunity to expose Lesley for the liar that she was, but then she realised that Florence no longer cared. She could see that her sister-in-law had healed her wounds and was now able to move on with her life.

Eileen knew that there would be no need for her to rush any decisions that she had to make. She suspected that there would also be a respectful gap between the funeral and the wedding, giving her plenty of time before she moved into Florence's old house. She knew it was going to be difficult leaving Vic, but with the love and support of her family, she now felt it possible to do so.

With the service over, the family sombrely walked in the direction of the graveyard, Gerald slipped a comforting hand inside his mother's. The family made their way towards the grave sheltered under a huge tree and gathered around Charlie's final resting place. The villagers came in their droves to pay their respects, as they had for the butcher only days before. The Reverend Eastwick was in attendance and he praised Charlie Hughes for his services to the community and efforts in the war.

Gerald stood at the foot of his father's grave barely listening to the reverend's words. His mother would be married again soon to a man who they both loved and his cousins together with James and Michael would be coming to live here too. He stared once again into the deep crevice which housed the dead body of his father and felt sad about all the time he had lost. He loved his family dearly, but part of him still wished that he could have had the chance to say goodbye to Douglas and his dad.

"Are you coming Gerald?" Susan asked.

"No I think I am going to stay for bit longer," he replied. The gravedigger had almost finished filling the hole when Aggie tapped Gerald on the shoulder.

"Do you mind if I put this in with your dad?" Aggie asked showing Gerald the shoebox containing all her memories of her baby Hope. "I know your dad will look after her for me, you see," she said her eyes filling with tears, "because we need to think about this one's future now don't we," she continued stroking her belly gently and smiled joyously up at her husband. Gerald helped Aggie dig a shallow grave for the memories of the baby she had lost and then stood back to let the gravedigger finish his job.

Aunty Aggie had been on a long and difficult journey, he thought, as he watched her and his uncle walk hand in hand away from the graveside. He was pleased that they were having a baby. Although he knew that her damaged lungs made her weak and it was going to take all her strength to carry the child, he felt sure that this time all would be well. She had an attentive husband again, who would give her all the support and care that she needed, they were each other's rocks, of that he was certain.

All was quiet when the mourners had left the graveside, leaving Gerald a solitary figure standing over the grave of a man he never really knew. With tears of sorrow filling his eyes, Gerald regretfully turned to go but from amidst the gentle sound of the breeze there came the voice of someone he knew. Gerald slowly turned back to where he heard the voice calling and stood back in awe of the magnificent creature which stood before him. Resting on the top of the handle of the gravedigger's spade shone the startling green eyes of a magnificent red, white and blue striped butterfly.

Speechless at the sight of the amazing creature, Gerald waited. After a few moments the butterfly spoke again.

"I couldn't go without telling you how proud I am of you son," he said softly.

"I'm so glad you came back to see me. I thought I were never going to see you again," Gerald sobbed.

"I just wanted you to know son how much you was loved and that I were sorry that I haven't been in your life," the butterfly echoed.

Gerald moved closer to the remarkable creature, the familiar glow still emanating from his wings.

"Can't you stay with me?" Gerald begged.

"No my sweet boy, me time here has ended now but yours is just beginning, you have a family who love you dearly and I wanted you to see that Gerald. I will always love you son," the butterfly smiled, as he fluttered his wings and lifted into the blue summer sky.

"Dad?" Gerald said softly. "Thanks for giving me the chance to get to know you."

"It were a privilege to have had the chance Gerald," the butterfly replied. "I hope you'll never forget me," he whispered as he disappeared into the clouds.

"I never will, Dad, I promise you, I never will," Gerald called after him.

Gerald walked slowly away from his dad's graveside, knowing that a part of him would be in his heart forever now and joined his family waiting close by.

"You alright Gerald?" Florence cooed. Gerald wiped his teary eyes and slipped his hand gently into his mother's welcome grip. He smiled up at the man that was to be his new father and replied honestly.

"Yeh! Mam, I'm OK."

In the distance Gerald could see his cousins and old friends waiting for him and he rejoiced in the beauty of his extended family. He was thankful for what he had in his life and had come to accept the things that had shaped it, however difficult that may have been. Gerald thought about the time before Douglas had come into his life, how sad, alone and distanced from his family he had been. He had accepted that his dad wasn't ever coming back, but as he tightly gripped the wooden caterpillar in his pocket, he knew that he had a magic memory of him, one that he could treasure forever and for that he was so grateful.

Smiling to himself, he thought about all the tales he had told in the past, trying to make his life more eventful and interesting. He recalled the memories over the last 15 days of his summer holidays and realised that even without Douglas in his life, it was still so full of adventure. Every day magical things had happened around him. He had been blinded in the past and missed some of them, but from now on he was going to enjoy every moment.

The End